T0161313

THE MAN IN THE CARDBOARD MASK

SHORT STORIES BY ALVIN GREENBERG

The Man in the Cardboard Mask

Coffee House Press :: St. Paul, Minnesota :: 1985

"The Conservation of Matter" was first published by Fodder Editions (St. Paul) © 1983 Alvin Greenberg; "The True Story of How My Grandfather was Smuggled Out of the Old Country in a Pickle Barrel in Order to Escape Military Conscription" first appeared in *Black Ice*.

The publishers wish to thank the National Endowment for the Arts, a federal agency, for a Small Press Assistance Grant which aided in the publication of this book.

Cover drawing by Gaylord Schanilec.

Coffee House Press books are available from the publisher, and from Bookpeople, Bookslinger, Inland, Publishers Group West, and Small Press Distribution.

Coffee House Press
Post Office Box 546, West Branch, Iowa 52358

Library of Congress Cataloging in Publication Data

Greenberg, Alvin.
    The man in the cardboard mask.

    Contents: Where do folk sayings come from? –
The conservation of matter – The true story of how my
grandfather was smuggled out of the old country in a
pickle barrel in order to escape military conscription –
[etc.]
    I. Title
PS 3557.R377M3 1984   813'.54   84-15533
ISBN 0-918273-02-1

Table of Contents

THE MAN IN THE CARDBOARD MASK

Where Do Folk Sayings Come From?

A COUNTRY PROVERB where he lived commanded that "When the mice move into the house, a man moves out to his woodpile." Therefore, because he had trapped three mice in the kitchen already this week, he reluctantly accepted his obligation to get out there and start splitting logs before winter snapped shut on him all unawares. He didn't really feel like it – of all the chores moving to the country had brought his way, woodchopping was the one he liked least – but he didn't feel he had much choice in the matter, either. Not that he couldn't have bought a winter's supply of wood reasonably, even on the tight budget unemployment was forcing him and his wife to live on; they managed surprisingly well on her small salary, and there were plenty of other unemployed men around happy to cut, split, deliver, and stack at almost any price. And given how he felt about the task, he could even have taken the blow to his pride of having another man do a job he was perfectly capable of and clearly responsible for. No, what sent him out to the woodpile on this still-warm day was neither his pocketbook nor his ego, but a vague sense that, like it or not, he had simply better do what the conventional wisdom required of him. He accepted the fact that when hard times threw a community back on its own resources, it was natural to cling together by maintaining old traditions. He accepted the idea that, in precarious times like these, it probably wasn't advisable to take unnecessary risks. He also accepted the rather less comfortable feeling that attached to the proverbial advice was, somehow, an implied, but nonetheless forceful, "or else."

So he pulled on his old sweatshirt and a lumber yard cap and a pair of heavy work gloves, took his axe and wedge and maul out of the storage closet, and headed for the back yard. As he went, he remembered another saying he'd heard repeated several times recently – "Better to feed your children from an empty pot than shatter the bowl of ancient wisdom" – and it bothered him. Not that he had to worry about starving his children to uphold tradition, since he didn't have any. He and his wife lived alone in their small house in the woods among an ever-changing population of dogs and cats. It was just that there seemed to be something rather odd about that saying. For one thing, though he had never heard it before – not that he considered himself an expert on matters of folk wisdom – lately it seemed to be on everyone's lips. And for another, it seemed, well, rather self-serving.

He split logs for the next couple of hours in the soft, late-afternoon sunshine until his wife came home from work and he heard her calling him, from the kitchen doorway, above the thunk of the axe, "Jan, oh Jan!" When he lived in a medium-sized city in the south of the state, everyone called him Jan, with a *J* and a short, nasal *a;* but ever since he'd moved to the north country, people had begun to call him Jan, in the Scandinavian way, with a *Y* and an elongated, foreign *a,* Yahn, and even his wife had gradually slipped into that way of saying his name. It didn't particularly bother him. As he'd heard it said often enough, "Even the wisest philosopher will answer to Sooo, Piggie, when the bread is on the table." He just wondered at times why this change had occurred and what it meant. He'd had a high-school sweetheart who had devised a new and cuter variation on her name every year, but he would have been happy to remain Jan-with-a-*J* forever. For a while, after they had first moved north – they had come for the once plentiful jobs in the mines and forests—he had fought against the change, but he had soon realized it was a losing battle and succumbed. Clearly, there was a force at work over which he had no control.

He found Kathy in the kitchen, stirring up a great pot of spaghetti sauce. Her name had also undergone modification since their arrival years ago, the C with which she had always spelled it before gradually giving way to a K, first on casual notes sent to her by local friends, then on bills, eventually on payroll checks, bank statements, and even her driver's license, until now she even signed her letters to her mother with a K, and Jan himself felt that the K somehow suited her better. She looked up from her cooking, smiling, and explained that the reason she was making such a great quantity of sauce was that two other couples, friends from work, were coming for dinner. When Jan, sweaty and grimy from his wood cutting, said that in that case he'd better hurry to bathe and change before they arrived, she laughed and said, "Good luck, Jan, but you know how it is, 'No sooner is winter spoken of than the snow begins to fall.'" Jan laughed with her and turned to go, but before he was out of the kitchen the doorbell rang. Jan went to answer it, and as he held the door open to let both couples in—they had arrived simultaneously though in separate cars—he couldn't help letting the thought cross his mind that it was almost as if they had been summoned instantaneously by the saying that Kathy had uttered.

Never mind, he told himself as he got cold beers out of the refrigerator for the guests, soon the job market will improve and I will have work again and I won't spend my time sitting around brooding about such things, by next summer for sure. As soon as he saw the company settled around the kitchen table with their beers, and talking with Kathy as she cooked, he went to wash his hands and face and put on a clean shirt. The dinner went nicely, even though much of the discussion concerned the scarcity of work for the men and the poor pay. That condition had gone on for

3

so long now, however, that most of the bitterness had been drained from it. An editorial that had appeared in the weekly paper not long ago had cautioned that "If you only eat rocks, you will soon find it hard to rise from the table," and the men had all discussed this many times since and found that they were in total agreement with it, though it had occurred to Jan, even if he refrained from saying it, that if it hadn't been for the clerical and service jobs available for their wives, they would soon have had nothing *but* rocks to eat. But never mind, Jan told himself once more, we will not even put pebbles on the plates around here, at least so long as there is company in the house.

Later, when the company was gone and Kathy was seated at the kitchen table, her lap full of cats, talking with Jan while he did the dishes, she wondered aloud why he had been so quiet at dinner. "I hope you're not thinking about moving back to the city," she said. "Everyone thinks about moving to the city," Jan told her. It was the most frequent topic of conversation whenever any of the men got together, on the few day-labor jobs that became available or at the hardware store or at the tavern where they could rarely afford to go anymore. The city was opportunity, jobs. "But it's all talk," Kathy objected, "nobody knows that for sure and besides, nobody ever goes." It wasn't that they didn't want to go, Jan reasoned as he scrubbed the pots, more that they seemed reluctant to leave here, almost afraid. Did Kathy recall the proverb that had been posted on the message board in front of the church this whole past month, in place of the usual biblical quotation that was changed weekly: The skunk that abandons the woods is soon only a bad smell on the highway to town. "And that frightens the men?" she asked. Jan didn't know how else to account for their fears. "I never knew the men around here took the church so seriously," she said. "Not the church," said Jan, "their lives." "And how does that make you feel, Jan?" she asked. He was just drying the last pot, the cast iron one she'd made the spaghetti sauce in. The big yellow lab was sleeping

4

between his feet. "Very tired," he said, "much too tired to think about going anywhere. I yoost vant to go to bed." Kathy laughed to hear him talk so funny, and all the cats scattered from her lap.

In the morning when he woke to find Kathy already gone and a heavy rain falling, Jan felt deeply troubled on two counts. For one thing, he had always been a light sleeper, and never before had Kathy slipped out of bed ahead of him in the morning without his being aware of it, without him leaning over to give her a hug or caress her back as she sat for a moment on the edge of the bed. For another, even as he lay there in the empty bed listening to the rain mumbling on the roof, he had a vague sense that there was something that he didn't know that he ought to know, that he had better know before the day was over. By the time he was dressed and sitting on a kitchen chair lacing up his boots, he knew what it was that he didn't know, and that left him feeling all the more troubled. There was a saying about days of heavy rain after a long dry spell at the end of summer, only he couldn't remember how it went. One of the rhymed ones, he thought, trying out some of the common rhythms in his head, days of heat, days of rain, da da ta, da da ta, that wasn't right, he couldn't quite seem to come up with it and then to top it off one of the leather thongs he used as bootlaces snapped as he pulled it tight. Whistle at the cow, get bit by the sow, he thought, looking at the strand of leather in his hand and wondering where that came from. He had never worked around animals in his life.

He let the broken piece drop to the floor, pulled the coffeepot over and poured himself another cup, and was staring deeply into it as if somewhere in its swirling surface lay the secret to the rhythm that held the secret to the words he knew he'd better remember soon so he could get on with doing whatever the conventional wisdom said he'd better be doing on a day of rain after a long dry spell at the end of summer, when suddenly the kitchen door slammed behind him. He looked around to see Kathy standing

5

there, peeling out of her dripping slicker, smiling broadly at him, her long golden brown hair damp and twisted. He hadn't realized there was so much gold in her hair, and he wondered, for a moment, if it had always been that way. But when he spoke it was to ask her what she was doing home so early. "Oh, Jan," she said, laughing, "it's Saturday, I just went over to have coffee and sweet rolls with Solfred, look what I brought you back." She held out a plastic bag with two caramel rolls in it, but instead of taking it Jan reached down and picked up the broken leather thong. "It isn't Saturday," he said. And who is this Solfred, anyway, he wondered, twisting the strip of leather around his fingers. "Of course it's Saturday, silly," she said, starting to hum a little tune softly as she took a plate out of the cabinet and set the two rolls on it and placed it in front of Jan and turned to get the butter for him. "No, I'm sure there's at least one day to go before Saturday," said Jan, "it can't be Saturday yet, how do you know it is? What's that you're humming?" Kathy stood in front of the refrigerator with the butter dish in her hand and sang:

> *Monday through Friday*
> *Sweet sunshine wants to play;*
> *When the rain begins to fall*
> *You know it's Saturday.*

It had an awfully familiar ring to Jan. "That's how you know today is Saturday?" he asked. "Sure," she said, "just look out the window."

Eventually, Jan tied together the broken lace and went outside to chop wood in the rain, leaving the two caramel rolls untouched. He was soaked through in minutes, the wooden axe handle kept slipping in his hands, and the heavy blade made only a dull thunk when it struck the logs instead of the crisp ring he wanted to hear, but he kept at it all the same. He couldn't see why it had to be Saturday just because it was raining; since when did the weather dictate which day of the week it was? He knew the old saw that claimed that "A man is like a guitar: if he does not tune himself to the weather, the weather will soon leave him unstrung," but he thought that this was just carrying things too far. He chopped and chopped and chopped, pausing only to toss the split logs onto the growing pile and to lift a whole one onto his block. Finally he stopped, puffing and leaning on his axe, still feeling that something unjust was at work here. "Dammit," he said aloud, "the calendar is a human invention, it doesn't have a damned thing to do with the rain." Hearing his own voice so suddenly in the midst of the steady hiss of the rain startled him and he fell silent, like a man who has blasphemed in church, almost expecting to be struck by a bolt of lightning. There was a sudden heavy rumble behind him and he swung about, axe in hand, to see the pickup truck pulling to a stop at the end of his gravel driveway. The driver climbed out, under a wide-brimmed cowboy hat that shed the downpour on all sides, waving and calling across the yard to him: "Hey, Jan, what kinda way is that to spend a rainy Saturday?"

Olson wanted to watch the Saturday afternoon football game on TV, but Kathy and Jan didn't have a TV and Olson, who lived in an old log cabin in the woods, didn't even have electricity, and none of them wanted to spend any money to watch the big-screen TV down at the One Pine Bar & Lunge – the *o* in Lounge on the sign outside had been missing so long that a whole generation had grown up in town that talked about going "down t' the Lunge" – so they sat at the kitchen table and drank coffee instead and listened to the week's worth of gossip that Olson had brought. Olson's cowboy hat, on the counter beside the stove, dripped and steamed, until Jan, his mind wandering in the steamy intricacies of Olson's tales, began to believe it was raining harder inside than out. Kathy filled and refilled their cups with steaming coffee. She had even gotten her grandmother's glass cups out for the occasion. Jan, holding his cup before his eyes, could see Olson's face quite clearly

7

through the thin brew and thought, It is no thicker than the steam that rises from it. Olson finished telling the story about how shocked the Lutheran minister had been when he found out why Nils Pederson, the carpenter, had bought a cow, and was steaming right along without a pause into the terrible business about the Helgerson boy and the Helgerson girls, the two cousins, that is, when Jan began to wonder how come Olson, who lived alone twenty miles out of town in the woods without a telephone, hadn't worked in years, never attended church, and didn't have any friends to speak of, knew all this up-to-the-minute gossip. If the air in the room hadn't been so thick with moisture that he felt he might drown if he opened his mouth, Jan would have asked him. Instead, he sat and sipped his coffee and watched Olson's face, which gleamed as if it were covered with sweat though Jan knew it was only condensation from the steam in the room, while Olson told them what happened when the Sheriff's car broke down way out on County Road Q last night and he left his wife in the back seat handcuffed to the runaway Olsen kid – no, no relation, Olsen with an *e* – while he hiked back into town for help. And again, this very morning, in spite of all the warnings Sorenson had given him, there was the dumb Finn who ran the florist shop delivering flowers his very own self to Sorenson's wife. To say nothing of what the UPS truck had come all the way out from the city to deliver to Nora Carlstrom last Tuesday. Kathy laughed and spilled the coffee she was pouring. Jan, watching it run steaming off the edge of the table and onto his leg, was surprised to find that it didn't burn. Must be because it's so thin, he thought. Olson stopped just long enough to lift his cup so Kathy could sponge up underneath it and then started talking about why his divorced daughter, who lived in town, liked to get both of the Torgerson girls over to babysit even on Saturday nights like tonight when she *didn't* drive over to Round Lake to the movies, but Kathy, squeezing out her sponge into the sink, finally interrupted to ask him how he managed to know all

8

that stuff, considering. Instead of answering, Olson looked up at Kathy and said, "Solfred tell you 'bout Earl comin' over in the middle of the night?" Oh, thought Jan, *that* Solfred, but then he realized he didn't know why he thought that. Who was Earl? Who were the Torgersons? Who were all of these people? Who was he? Jan wondered. "I'd even tell you 'bout *him*," Olson said, chucking his thumb at Jan, "if there was anything to tell, but most days it seems to me there's purt near nobody home there." He laughed. Jan laughed. Kathy laughed but she also repeated her question: "But how do you know, Olson?" Olson tipped his chair back and plucked his cowboy hat off the counter. "I don't rightly know how I know," he said, shaking his hat so that a fine spray rained across the room, "that's just the way it is, is all. I don't ask, it just comes to me. Like they say, I guess, 'nothin' bidden, nothin' hidden.'" He stood up and plunked his hat down on his head. "Guess I'd better go look to my dogs." "You mean you don't know what they're doing?" Jan teased. "Oh, I know," said Olson, "that's why I'd best be goin'." "Come see us again soon, Olson," said Kathy, walking with him to the kitchen door. "Yeah," said Jan, still seated at the table, "especially if you know what's going on here."

"I swear," said Kathy when Olson was gone, "I think he makes up half of that stuff. Did you hear what he said about his own daughter?" She was walking around the kitchen with her hands in her jeans pockets, giggling. "Probably thinks he has to entertain us for having him in for coffee." "Who were those people, anyway?" Jan asked. He still sat in his chair at the kitchen table with the piece of leather lace that had come untied again, twisting and untwisting it around his fingers. "Oh Jan, don't be silly, those are your neighbors." "Don't have any neighbors out here," Jan mumbled, tugging at the thong, "don't have any friends, don't have any relatives, don't have any work." He had one end of the leather strip wrapped around the first two fingers of his left hand and was tugging and tugging at the other end with his right hand, but it wouldn't give. "Can't even remember what I'm supposed to be doing today." "Oh Jan, you are in a funny mood today." Kathy stopped her pacing and sat down across the table from him. "You'll feel better soon. It's almost hunting season. You'll like being out in the woods with your rifle and the dogs and the deer." At the word "deer," the yellow lab that had been sleeping under the table lifted its head and whined softly. "But I don't hunt," cried Jan, "I've never hunted." Do I? he wondered. Have I? He couldn't recall that he had ever owned a gun, but he didn't at all like that way the dog had whined when Kathy said "deer." Maybe it was just coincidence. He looked under the table and saw that the yellow dog was asleep again, its head on its paws. Obviously it was not expecting anything to happen soon. Thank goodness, thought Jan, I need a little time to figure this out. Kathy reached across the table and took his hands to stop him from tugging at the thong. "It's still raining," she said. "Of course," he said, "it's still Saturday." "Oh Jan, you're so serious about everything these days." "Ya, sure," he said, "Seriously confused. Ooof da." She took both his hands, the thong still wound around his fingers, into hers. "Make love with me," she said. For a moment, he didn't quite understand what she was talking about, even though she was standing by then, pulling him up from his chair. Then he remembered. Of course: The long dry summer ends in rain, bringing husband and wife together again. We'd better do this, he thought, letting her lead him out of the kitchen, or we could be in a lot of trouble. He wasn't sure how anyone would know whether or not they had obeyed this particular piece of wisdom, but he wouldn't have taken the chance. Wasn't there always an Olson around?

Later that evening, after they had warmed up the leftover spaghetti for their supper, they got a call from Olson. "Where are you calling from, Olson," Jan heard Kathy saying, "you don't have a phone." Olson was in town, his truck wouldn't start though he'd been fiddling with it for over an hour, and he'd finally broken into the drugstore to use the phone since nothing else was open except the Bar & Lunge and he didn't want to go in there because he didn't drink anymore and it was still raining and except for his daughter he didn't know anybody who lived in town. Kathy looked up questioningly at Jan, her hand over the mouthpiece of the phone, as she relayed all this to him. "Might as well," Jan shrugged, "there's nothing much else to do around here what with the deer season still a month off." The rain was beginning to let up by the time they reached town, much to Jan's relief, because he found handling the pickup a terrific strain. It felt as if he had never been behind the wheel of a pickup before; he couldn't get accustomed to its height and feel, though Kathy kept assuring him that he'd always driven it like a man born with cowshit on his boots and a gun rack behind his head. He didn't dare take his eyes off the dark, slick road long enough to turn around to see if there really was a gun rack behind him. It was enough to read the vehicle's high mileage in the glow of the dashboard lights. You can't really know another man, he understood, until you have driven a thousand miles in his truck. But just look at all the thousands of miles on this thing, he thought, as he caught a glimpse of Olson standing at the corner waving at them, obviously recognizing the truck even in the dark, and who is this man I have not yet gotten to know?

Olson spent the night with them, sleeping flat out on his back on the living room floor with all his clothes on, even his boots, but Jan couldn't sleep at all. First he thought about standing out in the rain on Main Street, going over Olson's old Ford pickup more by feel than by sight, since the streetlights at either end of the block were shattered. He had checked out the system step by step while Olson and Kathy sat talking in the cab of the truck, until he found the cracked distributor cap and realized there was nothing they could do about it in the middle of the night. Even if they got the distributor dried out and the engine started, it would konk out before Olson got halfway home. But leaving Olson stranded on a dark highway didn't bother Jan half so much as his own success in figuring out the nature of the problem. Olson, at least, had probably had that sort of experience before. Might as well ask a moose to do math as expect a city boy to keep things running on his own, thought Jan. After all, hadn't he always hurried to the nearest service station at the first sign of anything going wrong with his car? He *thought* he had. No, he was sure he had. At least he hadn't actually fixed Olson's car, that was some relief, though suddenly a whole string of options occurred to him whereby he might have managed to do so temporarily. No, he thought, trying to push them away like bad dreams, I don't know these things, I am from somewhere else, I am not from where all these things are from. "Help," he called softly, feeling like the moose who could not make things add up, "help." Kathy stirred beside him in her sleep, but he didn't see any point in waking her, she couldn't help him, she was from the same place he was from, wherever that was. Probably, he thought, the same place the unmathematical moose was from. Yes, he wondered, where *did* that moose come from? Kathy turned over again and muttered something he couldn't make out, almost as if she were answering his question. He started to say "What?" but checked himself; even if she were to wake up and speak clearly, he wasn't sure he wanted to hear it.

Just before dawn, when the conventional wisdom told him he would fall asleep at last, Kathy threw off the blankets she had kept pulled up to her neck all night, and the sudden warm fragrance of her body, like the yeasty odor of baking bread, made Jan realize he was too hungry to fall asleep now. He slipped carefully out of bed, pulled on jeans and a flannel shirt and a pair of woolen socks, and went out to the kitchen, stepping carefully over Olson's prone body, which he located more by sound than sight, as he crossed the living room. Olson was snoring roughly, in an erratic, absent-minded sort of way, no rhythm at all to it, and Jan was surprised that he hadn't been hearing him all along.

He had always heard how precious such a time as this was, to have a house all to yourself in the early morning dark. Granted, he still carried the warmth of Kathy's smell with him, and Olson's snore still fumbled after him, but in spite of all that, he was, he knew, essentially alone here. In the pitch-black darkness of the kitchen, he found the refrigerator easily, and when he opened it the light, long since burned out, did not come on, but suddenly, in the frosty draft that enveloped him, he understood how Olson knew all those things. Knowledge, he said to himself, is just like that. He remembered how his mother had prized having the house all to herself in the morning before the rest of the family awoke, remembered a time when he had startled her in the kitchen, coming in for breakfast on a still-dark winter morning and turning on the light and not expecting to find her seated at the kitchen table, jumping as if she had been surprised by a burglar. He reached into the back of the second shelf of the refrigerator and put his hand at once on the jar of instant coffee. Knowledge, he thought, is like a potato: you don't even know it's hiding under the ground until your hunger takes you to it.

He ran his hand over the instant coffee jar as if he were brushing crumbs of earth from it. For sure, he thought, I will make a garden next spring, like I have always wanted to do. Though he did not know, moving soundlessly around the dark kitchen repeating the promise of a spring garden to himself, that that was what he had always wanted to do, he nonetheless knew that that was right. He laid his hands easily on the enamelled saucepan, filled it with cold tap water, set it on the range, picked the box of matches off the back of the stove, and lit the burner. Only just now, he realized, in the dark, did he discover what it was he had always wanted to do. No, he thought, what it is I am doing. Now he had the soft blue glow of the burner, which illuminated the solid outlines of refrigerator and stove and countertop, to help him as he found a cup and a spoon, spooned the instant coffee into the cup, added half a spoonful of sugar, put the coffee jar back in the refrigerator and got the milk out. Why, he thought, I am not especially smart, I have always known that, but I could have gone through life stupid as well had I not come up against this need to know what I am doing, which could only have happened to me here, and not back where we came from where I always took whatever I was doing for granted. Of course, I am just the same, but now I am one of the lucky ones because I have learned to know what I need to know even if I do not know how I know it. I will never have to feel quite so stupid again. By now his water was boiling, so he quickly turned off the burner and, plunged once again into the heavy dark, found a hotpad to lift the pan off the range and filled his cup with the boiling water, set the pan back down, added his dash of milk, returned the carton to the refrigerator, stirred the coffee gently, and then placed the spoon quietly in the sink. By god, he thought, when at last he sat down at the kitchen table to sip carefully at the hot coffee, I did this in the dark. It wasn't much, he knew—how many cups of coffee did he drink in a day, after all—but he did it in the dark. The things a person could do!

The Conservation of Matter

1.

WATCHING THE WAKE of the boat roll out, spreading to touch the low banks on both sides of the channel, only reminded Wilson of how much he always preferred looking at where he'd been. So he turned and walked forward, stepped down into the enclosed cabin with the others, and – not looking around at all, making it clear that he wasn't choosing a place next to any of them in particular – sat down at the first open spot he saw on the low bench. From there the only view of the outside was a view up, through the small windows, to a brilliant summer sky, a few gulls circling, a brown pelican chuffing heavily along on a parallel course not far above, keeping just abreast of the boat.

Inside the cabin they all sat with their heads lowered. Not one of them had so much as glanced up at Wilson when he entered and stood there for a moment in the doorway, half waiting for some brief look of recognition and wholly aware that he was not going to get it, that they knew he was there without looking, that there was no one else it could have been. Even now they all sat with their eyes focused on the luggage and equipment stacked between and around their feet. At the far end of the cabin the man running the boat – Wilson did not know his name, having seen him only once before, many weeks back, on the trip out to the island – was going through the bag of outgoing mail on the floor at his side. Keeping one hand on the wheel, he was leaning over and pulling mail out of the leather satchel with the other and stacking it in a neat pile on the seat beside him. Wilson was shocked to see that every time he pulled out one of the picture postcards that Susan had made up for them, he flipped it over and glanced at the message on the other side. There were several letters of his own in there, Wilson remembered, written and deposited in the satchel earlier in the week, safely sealed but suddenly outdated by events. He would arrive home before them. He considered going up to the front of the cabin and retrieving them from the pile, but he didn't.

Instead, he looked at the woman sitting next to him, saw that she was not looking back at him, looked up out the window across the cabin and saw that the pelican had pulled slightly ahead of the boat, looked down at his own feet and the empty space between them, looked over at the woman again. She was still not looking at him.

"Joanie?" he said.

She was in her early forties, square-faced, thick auburn hair pulled back tight, chin buried in the open neck of her blue work shirt. Wilson saw her now as one of the sad, angry children orphaned by the revolution. After a little while, she moved her head from left to right, almost imperceptibly, then repeated the gesture, eyes still firmly fixed on the floor: Leave me alone.

When he looked away from her he saw that Sarah, on the opposite bench, was watching him, eyes fierce and narrow in her dark face, a menacing squint. Another one, thought Wilson. He could not recall that he had ever seen Sarah smile, though he knew he had never heard her raise her voice, either. He remembered reading about gangs of orphaned children who roamed the ruined cities of Europe after World War II, cornering unwary adults who wandered into their territory of bombed-out basements and debris-choked alleys, circling them with blank eyes and thin, unsmiling faces, setting upon them with teeth and nails if necessary, often with the youngest at the head of the pack, taking what they wanted, what they needed, what was there. Wilson still did not know what they wanted from him.

Suddenly Sarah smiled at him. Not much of a smile, just a small, abrupt turning up at the corners of her mouth, a few lines creasing her young face, a white glimmer of teeth, an even tighter squint compressing her blue eyes. And Wilson, about to return her smile, quickly pulled back on his impulse as he watched a tiny bubble erupt from the corner of her mouth and burst at once on her lower lip and, in that brief moment, recognized her smile for what it was: a smile of victory, the satisfaction of a small carnivore, a young bobcat perhaps, at the culmination of its first successful hunt, aware that it has its prey cornered. As he looked back at her, stiffening his lips, her smile slowly broadened and became fuller, more real; her lips parted and he knew that she had watched his own smile collapse, had observed the shadow of enlightenment crossing his face. Now she sat up, erect, shoulders back, head tipped back against the wall, black hair fanning out and over her shoulders, arms crossed over her t-shirt, just below her breasts. He couldn't hold her gaze.

Looking forward, out the front windows of the cabin, beyond the man at the wheel, who held it loosely in both hands and now wore a dirty white yachting cap Wilson had not seen before, he spotted the pelican well out ahead of the boat. It looked as if it were guiding the boat down the long, straight channel toward the mainland dock at its far end, still out of sight because of the low lay of the land and the tipped-up prow of the boat. Wilson wondered why it was doing that, why a pelican would follow the same path as the boat, a straight line toward an unseen, distant point. Why, he wondered, were any of them doing it? They didn't have to leave the island, in spite of what had happened. No one had told them they had to go, and he was at a loss to know how this mutual agreement had been reached and how he had become a part of it, though he also knew it would have been impossible, pointless, for him to stay on without the rest of them. He did not understand them, though: how it was that, finally, they had all just packed and carried everything they could down to the dock without a word being said and found the boat waiting for them, the heavy inboard motor idling and the two men who worked for the project, the one now at the wheel and the other who remained behind, waiting to cast off. Terrible things happened everywhere, all the time. But you still had to go on. That did not mean that you were ignoring what had happened: quite the contrary; it meant that otherwise what was the point of ever beginning anything. Ever. But this Wilson did not understand: this tacit agreement to leave, all of them quietly stowing their own belongings and the lighter project equipment, whatever they could carry, in the cabin and then coming back out on the open rear deck to stare at him where he still stood on the dock, until at last Howard said his name, "Charlie," just like that, flat, no emotion, and Carolyn arched her hand out over the gunwale, and he took it and allowed himself to be led aboard. He had not brought any luggage; all his belongings, not even packed, still occupied the room in the mansion where he had been living for most of the month.

He had an urge to go back out on the open deck now, to stand there in the hot sun and the humid offshore breeze looking back at the island, even though he knew that by now it would be indistinguishable in the distance from the low, marshy shorelines of the other islands that bordered the channel. He kept his seat on the bench, though, sensing that almost anything he did right now would be taken as an affront. Especially looking back. It occurred to him for a moment that they might have been prepared to depart without him, but as he thought about it he knew otherwise: that they were waiting for him, that they had no intention of leaving without him, that they knew he would join them at the dock and allow himself to be led aboard without resistance. He was theirs now. For what, he didn't really know. Forever, maybe, he thought.

But he also didn't know which of them could be so naive now as to think that it was possible to get what they wanted – from him, from themselves – or to get to wherever they thought they were headed now, without ever raising their eyes from the floor, without ever looking back. Wasn't there anyone among them who knew that that was what mattered, that that was what they had to do, and keep doing, and keep doing.

Maybe only Sarah, he thought, maybe she was young enough to dare once she outgrew her anger. Maybe the anger itself would force certain obligations on her she wasn't even aware of yet. Maybe. But for now Sarah only looked across at him, not back, still smiling. And her smile made him feel even more desperate to break away, to shake himself free from its fierce containment, to show them he didn't belong in here with them, maybe none of them did, to demonstrate his own necessity, the importance of going back out there and standing on the open, sun-baked deck, looking back toward, for, the island.

He dropped his eyes to the empty wooden flooring between his feet, clenched his fist in his lap, and heard a voice from the front of the cabin say, "Take it easy, Charlie, we're almost there."

It was Steven, standing beside the man at the wheel, straddling the empty mail satchel, hands in his pockets, surveying the cabin, and Wilson wondered where he thought he had gotten the right to stand up there like that and speak for them. Hadn't that been settled already? The women hated *him* worst of all. None of them looked around at him. Not even poor Howard. Wilson looked away, beyond Steven, out the front window again, and saw that the pelican must have outdistanced them. It was no longer in sight. Then he let his eyes wander back to Steven again, though he still only wanted to look back out the other way: back toward the island which, he thought, could never really be out of sight now, ever, could it? It was so densely populated, so full of what mattered: you could not, he felt, leave something that densely populated behind, not ever – no matter where you thought you were going. The past was seething with life and nothing they could do to him would change that. He did not really think they meant to do anything to him, but he felt that even if they did it wouldn't change anything. Not anything that mattered. They could do something very simple to him, something very final, but what mattered was always very complex, he knew, and never final. You could not alter what truly mattered, regardless of what you did; it was just the other way around: what mattered altered everything else. That was why you cared, in spite of everything. Why you ever began anything and why you kept on, too.

That was what called you to action sometimes, too, led you to say what you might not otherwise say, while everyone else kept their heads down: that need to clear the way to let what mattered truly matter. If you wanted to do that, Wilson decided, you could not let the assholes take charge because they would obliterate everything. In the kingdom of the assholes you would not be allowed to look back, only ahead, out the front windows, at the sun-bleached, empty sky. The assholes were assholes because of never looking back, never holding to what mattered. Because they always stood at the front ordering you to take it easy. Thinking that was all there was to it. What the women wanted was something else, but this, Wilson knew, he could not allow.

"Sit down, Steven, and shut your fucking mouth," he said, his hands still clenched in his lap, "or I'll kill you, too."

2.

The orange and blue helicopter perched cautiously on the hard-packed sand of the beach at the far end of the island, its slowly turning blades rustling nervously. To Wilson they gave off an added anxiety, a sense of someone's unspoken fear that to turn off the engine would be to risk not being able to take off from the island again. Wilson sat alone, on a driftwood log polished almost pure

20

white, having carefully aligned his position with that of the helicopter to block his view of the group further up the beach. But now he could see that it must have broken up, for several of the men were coming around the rear of the helicopter, walking single file, close to the water's edge. None of the women.

As they passed the helicopter one of the men, uniformed, stooped and circled around to the front. He reached up and opened the door, and Wilson saw that someone else, also uniformed, probably the pilot, had remained inside all this time. The man on the ground seemed to be saying something to him, then closed the door and, still stooping, scuttled ahead to join the end of the line that was heading down the beach now toward Wilson. There were four of them, two uniformed and two not, three strangers and one not. Howard.

Ever since arriving on the island they had seen the helicopters overhead fairly regularly, just like this one, perhaps this same one. It was impossible to ignore the ugly, heavy coughing of their low passes overhead. The rumor was that they were patrolling the islands and the inlets for drug smuggling, which made sense to Wilson considering all he had read in the papers about the extent of the problem along the southern coast here. But he thought it odd that they only patrolled by day, never by night, which seemed to him to be the obvious time for any sort of smuggling activities. The low passes they made over the island several times a day were a disturbance to everyone's work, and Wilson felt that, even set here more quietly upon the beach, its rotor flapping, the helicopter's was an edgy, disturbing presence, almost as bad in its own way as what lay further up the beach, blocked by the helicopter from his view.

Only he knew that nothing was worse than that. That that was irremediable. That the helicopter would eventually lift off the beach in its small whirlwind of sand and noise and go away, but *that:* they would be marked by that forever.

He looked up into the sudden shade of the three men standing over him and wondered whether he ought to stand up to meet them at their own level with the responses they were going to demand of him, but he kept sitting. Howard, he could see through the gap between the two uniformed officers, had come to a stop about twenty feet back and was just standing there, not even looking at them, shuffling his feet, eyes on the sand, as if he were hunting for shells. Beyond him Steven was just coming into sight from around the rear of the helicopter, taking long strides now on a direct line toward Howard. In the bright light, at this distance, Steven's reddish gold hair and beard blended so fully into his sunflushed face that Wilson found it impossible to make out his expression. Howard's, under the shadow of his tennis hat, was probably sullen, and Wilson, looking up, was certain that the Lieutenant's was being kept deliberately blank. Expressionless, Wilson thought, and he did not even need the heavy anonymity of the goggle-type sunglasses the other two wore; he could do it just with his eyes.

"Tell me a little more about your part in it, Wilson," the Lieutenant said. Wilson hesitated, trying to recall the Lieutenant's name, then decided it didn't make any difference. It didn't make any difference that they had already talked for an hour or more at the mansion before coming back down here, the police in the helicopter and the rest of them in the van, which was parked just out of sight over the dunes now. It didn't make any difference that he must have heard the Lieutenant's name half a dozen times or more. The Lieutenant was a stranger, all three of these men were strangers, they would always be strangers and this had nothing to do with them. This didn't even mean anything to them; it was just an ordinary part of their job. Wilson didn't want to know any of their names.

He still sat on the white driftwood trunk. He said, "I already told you, I just . . ."

"I don't mean that," said the Lieutenant, "I mean your part in the whole project."

"Oh," said Wilson. He almost felt he ought to rise to respond, it was such a formal sort of question, there was such a history to the answer.

"I am the humanist," he said, looking up into the Lieutenant's shaded face. "I am the fly in this scientific web, or, if you prefer, the pickpocket in this community of scientific trust." He was quoting himself at his most humanistically cynical from a dinner table conversation of several nights ago, and he knew it was the wrong tone. But he didn't know any right tones. Letting his eyes drop, he could see that Steven had come up to where Howard was standing now and had grasped him sharply by the elbow.

"Look, Lieutenant," he continued, "I am really just here to observe. These people are scientists, they have a specific project to carry out in the field here, they have a set of objects to study in the natural world. I just came along to watch, to see how it is they go about doing what they do. You know about the turtles, Lieutenant?"

"I know about the turtles," the Lieutenant said.

Wilson wondered how much he really knew about the turtles, even if he had grown up along this coast, where the big sea turtles came ashore to lay their eggs in the sand at the very spot where they themselves had been hatched years before. The turtles were the reason they were here, the reason the State had given them permission to reopen for their use the old mansion that had been closed up ever since the island had been willed to the Wildlife Commission, the reason they were being allowed to spend the summer doing research here. And they had been there already in the night, hidden behind the dunes, when the big turtles had clambered up onto the beach out of the sea to mate and bury their eggs in the sand; they were to be there again when the eggs hatched and under a starlit sky the young turtles scampered across the beach and into the safety of the waiting ocean. They were there to study the mysterious workings of the celestial imprint, that pattern of stars in the night sky that the baby turtles carried with them into the sea as an inner map that in future years they would follow back to this very same spot where they had been hatched.

"Well," said Wilson finally, "they watch the turtles. I watch them."

"That's what you call a humanist," said the Lieutenant.

Wilson looked up again. "A humanist," he said. "I found the body."

The Lieutenant was staring down at him, hands on hips. The two uniformed officers at his right were standing in exactly the same posture, though Wilson could not see, through their dark glasses, what their eyes were doing. Beyond them Steven was still gripping Howard's elbow tightly, and the two of them, motionless, seemed to be staring in his direction. Beyond them, the fluttering helicopter: and suddenly Wilson saw that what had attracted his attention to that direction was not the flash of sunlight off the slowly turning rotors but the four women who had just emerged around the rear of it to stand right at the water's edge, where the gentle summer waves just crept up over their feet. They were totally nude. What shocked Wilson was not their nudity – there had been plenty of hot afternoons when all of them had stripped off their clothes on this very beach and gone running into the sea together – but the fact that each of them seemed marked, just as she had been when he found her, with great splashes of blood across their bodies. Then Susan took a step forward and he saw, in the shifting light, that it was not blood but sand, that must have stuck to her sweaty skin when she kneeled or sat to remove her clothes. No, he thought, it was almost as if they had lain in the sand back there, rolled in it. He looked up. The Lieutenant was saying something to him, and he shook his head, trying to hear what it was. Steven and Howard stared at him, linked as before. Even the helicopter pilot stood leaning in the open doorway, looking down the beach at them as if awaiting instructions, clearly oblivious to the four women standing just behind his craft.

"What?" said Wilson.

The Lieutenant turned. The helicopter pilot waved at him, as if to remind him he was still waiting. The Lieutenant waved back, then lifted both arms and crossed them over his head. The women were gone.

When Wilson stood up, feeling suddenly dizzy from sitting in the bright, shattering heat, the Lieutenant turned around to speak to him again: "I said we'll take the body to the mainland with us now."

3.

"You did it, you know," Joanie said. Wilson realized that somehow, on the ride back, as all the others had fallen silent, she seemed to have come forward to speak for them.

"Can we please go inside now?" Wilson asked. He was so tired–so heavy, heavy tired–he felt as if he couldn't make it from the van into the house without someone's help, but he also knew that there was no way he could ask help of any of them right now. He looked at Howard. Carolyn had climbed down from the driver's seat and hurried into the house to crank up the radiophone as soon as they'd pulled into the drive, but the rest of them had just stayed there sitting in the van, and Wilson sensed that he had no choice but to do that too, at least until they gave him some sign that it was all right to do otherwise. Howard just lifted his eyebrows back at him: Don't look to me now. Steven, bigger, stronger, sat up straight in the front seat, and Wilson saw that by keeping his head high and his back to them he was trying to show that he was still in charge of what was going to happen here, just as he was nominal head of the project. But everyone else looked to Joanie for their clues.

"Do you know what I mean?" said Joanie. She was in the folding seat in the row in front of him, turned around to address him almost face to face. He couldn't get out of the van until she got up first and made room for her seat to be folded down so the three of them in the back seat, himself and Sarah and Susan, could exit. He didn't dare look over at Sarah, next to him. But he didn't think he had to respond to this, either. What did she think he was going to say? What did any of them think he was going to say? He was too tired to say anything. And hot. He felt too terrible to talk. He wanted to be helped down out of the van and allowed to go into the big, cool interior of the living room and just drop into one of the musty chairs there until the police came. The little bit of air that came through the side door of the van that Joanie had slid open as soon as they had come to a stop didn't help much.

Leaning forward, head down, Wilson gulped for air and asked again, "Please."

He heard the front door click and Steven say, "OK, I'll take care of this."

But before anyone could get out of the van, before the front door actually swung open or Wilson raised his head, he heard Joanie snap, "Sit!" and suddenly the van fell totally quiet again, no one moving.

Wilson was surprised at first at the abruptness of Joanie's authority. For the most part he had found her a diligent, quiet worker, seemingly anxious to prove that though the years had softened her body, she could keep up with any of them, including the men, in the physical work. And she had. She had hiked the island's beaches and worked on the fencing and been out in the sun from dawn to dusk, doing her cataloguing, filling one small notebook after another, but she had always done it with a sense of silent determination that had suggested to Wilson that she dared not squander any of her energies on words. She rarely even spoke at the dinner table or at their project meetings or even in the casual evening conversations. But Wilson remembered how he had wandered outside with her after breakfast their first full day on the island and found two strange dogs circling warily on the lawn. They were both big dogs, short-haired hunting types, brown and hungry looking, padding back and forth in front of them with their heads low. But Joanie had stepped right out toward them and given the same firm command she had just given Steven, and one of the dogs had sat at once, head up, tongue out, panting, obedient, as if waiting for her next command. The other had scampered off when she first spoke, out of sight around the corner of the house, but then returned, cautiously, and lay down in the shade of an oak far out on the edge of the lawn. Eventually, as she worked with the first dog, walking the lawn with it, ordering it to heel and sit and stay, the other approached too, followed at a little distance, never obeyed Joanie's orders but seemed to be watching to see how it was done. Now they were both house dogs. Joanie was certain they had been well-trained once, probably as hunters, and had been abandoned on the island either by poachers or when the house was vacated. They liked to lie on the cool flagstones in front of the fireplace–probably where they were right now, Wilson thought. One of them would sit or roll over for any of the group now, but the other still just watched.

Wilson watched Steven sit stiff and erect in the front seat now, not turning to acknowledge or challenge Joanie's order, though probably–Wilson could not be sure–with his hand still on the door handle. Next to him, Howard, who had been facing the back of the van a moment earlier, glanced up once at Steven's immobile head, then turned to face front and sat as motionless as Steven.

"OK," said Joanie, not even looking at them, her eyes on Wilson again, "that's good. Just keep it that way. You do what you're told and stay out of the way. You're not worth bothering with, either of you. This one back here, we know what he is. He's shit but he's what we want. But you two aren't even that, you're not even shit, you're not anything, you in particular, Steven, because you seem to think you're something." But she wasn't looking at Steven, not even at the back of his head, which he kept stiffly toward her. She kept her eyes on Wilson all the while.

"You're nothing," she continued, "nothing. Remember that. You and your little buddy up there are nothing, you are not even beneath contempt, you are at precisely the right level for contempt, but that is the level of a nothing. Understand? This back here, whatever he is, he is a something at least, something we're going to attend to at least, so you just leave us alone with this . . . this something, and maybe we'll leave you alone, too. Understand?" Joanie was looking at Wilson still as she asked the question, but he knew it wasn't a question she was asking of him, not just at that moment anyway. The van was silent.

"Speak!" she ordered, when a minute had passed and no one answered her last question.

"OK, OK," Steven said softly and quickly from the front seat. Howard, next to him, glanced over at him, then turned forward again and nodded.

Listening to all this, which somehow seemed terribly remote to him, almost as if it didn't concern him at all, Wilson realized it was the most words he had heard her utter at one time during all their weeks on the island. That it most certainly did concern him, he was well aware, if only from the way she kept her eyes on his face the entire time, and maybe, he thought, just maybe, now that she was talking, now that she was focusing on him even though she was not addressing him directly, not yet, maybe she would be willing to tell him just why it was that they were still sitting here in this hot, stuffy van in the midday heat in their pain and misery, just what it was she thought could be accomplished here, in this suffocating metal box. Just what she wanted of him.

He raised his head, sat up a little straighter, and asked her. He heard something at his left, from Sarah or Susan: a gasp, a whisper, he didn't know what it was, but he knew he couldn't turn and look, either. Joanie, in front of him, was still staring at him, eyes wider than before, mouth slightly open, as if she didn't believe it possible that he did not know what they wanted of him. It doesn't make any difference what she thinks, Wilson told himself, I haven't done anything, I can't do anything now, it doesn't make any difference what she wants if it's not anything I can do or give. If you want me to understand, he wanted to say to her, you have got to give me more help than this; there are not any commands that will get me to roll over with instant comprehension.

She looked, for a moment, in the face of his hard, unspeaking stare, as if she were about to say something. Her mouth opened wide, closed, opened again, but then instead of speaking she raised her right hand and snapped her fingers, spun around off the seat and jumped out of the van. Wilson could see the two men climbing down from the front, and then he leaned forward to fold down Joanie's seat and climbed out himself, Sarah and Susan right behind him. He stood there for a minute in the dirt driveway, feeling that even the direct noon sun wasn't as brutal as it had been inside the van, feeling the heat radiating from the van at his side, watching the others flow past him and on into the mansion. He was surprised to see that they had left the front door standing open for him, the cool, dark rectangle of its opening far more of an invitation than he would have expected. But as he started to take a step toward it, he heard a noise behind him and turned around. It was Susan, still in the doorway of the van, stepping down, sliding the door shut. It slammed. She started for the mansion, turning sideways as she passed him, keeping her eyes on him, turning backwards, still watching him, as she got to the other side of the drive.

"She's right, Charlie," she said, still watching him, still backing away toward the darkness of the open front door, "it's all your doing." She was small and her backward steps were precisely placed, as if she knew even without looking exactly where she was going.

"You're dead, Charlie," she said. Then she backed through the open door into the interior darkness of the hallway, and he couldn't see her anymore.

4.

"Charlie, help me."

"What is it?" He sat up quickly, fumbling for his glasses first and then the night-table lamp. The mansion was utterly silent, but the moment he switched the light on, the insects came beating loudly against the window screens.

"What is it?" he repeated. "Nancy, talk to me."

She said something, but it was so muffled he couldn't understand it, and he saw that she was lying face down, covers up over her shoulders though it was, as always, a hot night, and head buried under her pillow, so that all he could see of her were her two hands that pulled the pillow down on top of her head and the long strands of hair, grey and brown, that crept out from under the pillow.

"Hey," he said, reaching under the edge of the covers and sheet to rub her shoulders. He didn't want to try to move the pillow off her head, she seemed to be hanging onto it so desperately, but he wanted a better sense of where she was under there. "How can I help you if I can't see you? If you don't tell me what you want?"

"You can't help me," she said – or he thought he heard her say. Then she let go her grip on the pillow and he eased it off her head, saw that she was lying there with her face turned toward him, looking up at him with her eyes clear and dry.

"Jesus," she said, "What's that terrible noise?"

The night insects were beating their wings heavily against the screens. Some of them, Wilson knew, were as large as small birds. None of them was dangerous, but their size alone seemed unpleasant, that and the sense that they were always out there, waiting for a light to flash on, ready to come whirring madly against it, as close as they could get, their heavy bodies thumping again and again into the screens, the desperate rasping of their wings.

"We could turn the light out and talk," Wilson suggested.

"No," she said quickly, "leave it on." She sat up in the bed, reached over to the chair next to it for the cotton shirt she had been wearing earlier, then pulled it on and buttoned it up. In spite of the nagging, rasping flutter of the insects, Wilson thought she looked a little more at ease once she had the shirt on, so he said, "I'll help you, Nancy, if I can. You know that."

"Well, you can't," she said.

He looked over at his watch on the night table. It was nearly three-thirty. She was very clear, he thought, very precise especially in the way she made that last statement, for someone who had woken up crying for help at this hour of the night. Unless, he considered, she hadn't just woken up; he had been sleeping, but she might well have been lying there awake for a long time. Perhaps all night. Yes, he was sure of that, he could see it in how startlingly clear and wide open her eyes were.

"I want a cigarette, Charlie," she said. She was sitting straight up, not even leaning back against the headboard, reciting her list at him: "I want a cigarette, I want a drink, I want a sleeping pill, I want a tranquilizer, I want . . ."

She stopped. He was sitting up beside her now, reaching out to take one of her hands. There was no sound except for the continuous scraping and thumping of the insects against the screens. It never stopped for a second once a single light was on. They were killing themselves, Wilson realized, and he wanted the light off not for Nancy but for himself, not for the insects either, but for himself, because he didn't want to hear the sounds of such a terrible, mindless desperation.

"Frightened?" he asked. But it wasn't that she looked frightened to him; she looked too lucid, too much in control, if anything.

She nodded. She was pinching at her lower lip. Then she said, "Listen. Are you listening?"

"I heard you," he said.

She gestured at the window: "I don't mean me. I mean that, them. Jesus, they don't stop, do they? What do they want?"

"In."

"Ha." She pushed her pillow off onto the floor and lay back down, flat on her back, staring at the ceiling. He still held onto her hand.

"Do you want me to leave?" he asked. It was her room, after all.

"Do you want to leave?" She didn't even look at him as she asked it, but kept her eyes on the ceiling, as if that were where the terrible, ceaseless scraping of insect bodies was coming from.

"I like it here," he said. "I'm here because I like being here with you."

"Picked a winner, huh, Charlie?"

He leaned over her. "I'm at the rail," he said.

She only glanced at him briefly, then continued to look past him, straight up at the ceiling: "I don't hear you cheering."

"It's awful late," he said, "I don't want to wake the crowds, but I'm cheering. Don't worry."

"I never know what to do," she said, "with the people who look at your disaster and tell you not to worry."

"What disaster?" he asked.

"I'm not going to make it, Charlie," she said. "It's too late, there's too much that's happened, I'm too tired. I haven't got the staying power. I was raising kids, Charlie, while these people were raising their IQs."

"You're as smart as any of them. And just as competent."

"Only I'm in another race altogether, don't you see? Only no-body told the handicapper. To the handicapper, I'm just another horse, so on go the weights. But remember *just*, Charlie? What about the weights I'm already carrying? Jesus, there's such a toll it's taken. It doesn't leave you as much to go on with, you know? But I want to do it, Charlie, I think I can be good, I think I have something, but I don't know, I think it's too hard. I don't think I can do it."

32

"You do have something. You have the brains. You have the ability. You've already shown you can be part of this . . ."

"But sustain it, Charlie."

". . . and you're very lovely, too," he continued. He leaned over and kissed her forehead, surprised at how cool it was.

She continued to stare at the ceiling: "So?"

Wilson hated these pauses in the conversation. They were almost as uncomfortable as the conversation itself, because in them the whirring and thudding of the insects seemed to grow louder and louder still. At first he thought it was just that in the silence he could listen to them more closely, but then he decided that no, they really were louder, because there were more and more insects, and the longer the light stayed on the more came, there was no limit to their numbers, the night was full of them.

"It doesn't stop," she said. She was still staring at the ceiling, but he saw from the reflection of the light that her clear, brown eyes had grown moist, and he felt her squeeze back now with the hand he had been holding all this time. "It is one thing after another, and every one of them is always with you, there is nothing you can ever really leave behind, love, and yet it still doesn't stop. Every day still brings something else. Something old, something new, some *one* new, it doesn't make any difference. It's the weight, that's all it is, Charlie, the weight."

"I don't want to be any kind of burden for you," he protested.

"Oh, Charlie," she said. It was almost a laugh, and at last she turned her head slightly and looked over at him where he sat beside her: "Don't take it so personally, love. It's just me."

"Just you," he echoed, very softly.

"Mmmmm." She had closed her eyes, he saw, and her whole face had relaxed now, as if she had suddenly gotten very, very tired, as if she had suddenly let go of something very heavy. Still, in the silence, the insects came battering and scraping against the screens, wave after wave of them. She lay silent a long time and Wilson listened all that while, not knowing what to say himself, to the relentless, storm-driven surf of night insects lashing at the shore of the room.

Finally she spoke again: "You can turn off the light now, Charlie." And he reached over to flick off the small lamp on the nightstand.

"Let there be darkness," he said.

5.

He was sitting in the oversized living room in one of the musty old stuffed chairs, reading, when he saw Nancy coming down the grand staircase from her room on the second floor, so he closed his book and laid it down on the table beside him, with the others. Sarah was right at her elbow, and together they descended the stairs and crossed the living room toward him. He had been reading about snakes in several books, all of them heavy with mildew, that he had pulled off the bookshelf by the fireplace. The island – as they all knew from the beginning, when they had ordered snake bite kits for everyone – was reputed to harbor every variety of poisonous snake known in North America. Wilson had been amused to read, just moments ago, of an infallible sign for recognizing whether or not a snake was poisonous: the recessed venom pit in the front corner of the eye. What amused him was realizing that in order to so identify a poisonous snake you had to be so close to it that the knowledge was probably going to come too late to do you any good.

As they approached him, he stood up, nodded his agreement when Nancy suggested that he come with them into the dining room to see if their help was needed in setting up for dinner, then told them to go ahead, that he'd be right along as soon as he put the books away. He carried them across the room and put them back on the shelf carefully, one at a time, afraid their bindings might give and the pages tumble out. When he turned back he saw that Sarah was still there in the living room, watching him. He smiled at her but she didn't smile back, and as he came back across the room toward her she made no effort to step aside, no indication, no slight turn of head or body, to show that she was going to join him on his way to the dining room. She just stood there. So he stopped when he got to her and looked her directly in the eyes, suddenly aware that something was about to happen. She spoke almost at once.

"Just remember," she said, "you are responsible for everything you do." She was tall and lean, her long face framed by her spread of black hair, and he felt as if her words had a certain sinewy leanness to them also.

"Wait a minute, Sarah," he said carefully, wanting to find some way both to protest his innocence and to show respect for her intense sincerity at the same time.

"Just remember this," she continued, still staring right into his eyes, as if she hadn't even heard his brief interruption: "She isn't like the rest of us. She's had to fight for every inch of independence she's gained, and she's had to fight to hold that territory, too. Just like the rest of us. But she's a little older. A little more vulnerable. She's had more time for the soft spots to establish themselves before she went to war. Less time to build her defenses. Don't get me wrong: she's tough. Only she's not so tough as all that. Do you get me?"

"Sarah," he said. He wanted to take her hand, to reach out like that to talk to her, but he saw that her thin arms were stiff rods at her side and her hands tight little fists.

"Just tell me you understand what I'm saying," she said.

"You don't have to protect her from me," Wilson said.

"You'd better be right," she said. Then she turned, before he had any sense that she was prepared to move, and darted off toward the dining room, where he found her, by the time he arrived, already busy stacking plates on the buffet. Howard was just coming through the swinging door from the kitchen with a tray of water glasses, and Nancy, right behind him, carried the salad bowl. By the time Wilson had circled the table setting out the silverware, all the others had arrived, too, and Mrs. Halliday, who helped her sister in the kitchen, was carrying a heavy tureen to the buffet table. Fish again, thought Wilson.

"Fish again!" said Susan, popping up out of the chair she had sat down in to get out of the way of the pre-dinner flurry of activity. Wilson admired her liveliness. In fact, they had all praised her strange combination of boundless, seemingly nervous energy and an ability to sit nearly motionless for hours, as her work required, only her hands moving from time to time to change a slide or adjust the microscope or make a note on the pad beside her. To Wilson, though, Nancy's slow grace seemed even more amazing. Without rushing, she seemed to be able to do half again as much as most other people accomplished with great flurries of activity. As she crossed the dining room toward him now, he saw, beyond her, Mrs. Halliday setting out the rest of the food on the buffet, the bowl of rice and the platter of biscuits. Steven, nearby, was bending over to mutter something in Howard's ear, shaking his head and gesturing toward the buffet as he did so, but as usual he and Howard were first in line.

Sarah came through the serving line right behind Wilson, sat directly opposite him at the table, and seemed, he felt, to keep her eyes fixed carefully on him throughout the meal. She hardly seemed to blink or to look down at the food she was lifting from her plate to her mouth, and it made Wilson feel extremely self-conscious every time he brushed Nancy's hand, beside him, when he passed her the salt or butter, every time they bumped knees under the table or he turned to speak to her or smile at her. What was this? he wondered: this was a gathering of adults and there weren't going to be any secrets about their interactions, not for very long anyway, not in a group this small, but it was a group of mature

34

adults, their focus was on their work here and they certainly did not need anyone to keep watch over their personal lives: what they did, they did by their own choice. If there was anyone here whose job was to watch what they did it was his, Wilson's. And even in that case the purpose of his being there was not to pry into anyone's personal life or to study the interactions of a small social group in isolation. He was a humanist, not a psychologist or sociologist, and he was concerned with interdisciplinary research. His role was to examine the ways in which a group of scientists from diverse fields worked together on a complex research project. He only wished, at times, that he had more of a contribution to make to the progress of the actual project himself, aside from his willingness to contribute to the necessary physical labor. It amazed him, in fact, how much sheer physical work was involved in the project. He had studied interdisciplinary processes before, but this was the first time he had ever been out in the field with a research team, and he was glad that he had had the opportunity to come along because here, at least, with so many simple physical tasks to be done, he could be more of a participant, not just an observer.

Tonight he contributed what he had learned from his reading about snakes to the dinner table conversation. He told them what he had learned about the coral snake and the rattler and the water moccasin, their markings and habitats and behavior patterns, and was pleased that they allowed him to share this new-found information, even though he knew that there were undoubtedly several members of the group who, given their specialties, must have known considerably more about snakes than he had picked up in an hour's reading. He even forgot Sarah's watchful eyes on him as he held forth.

From the head of the table, at the far end, Carolyn arched her hand out over the table, fingers and thumb curved to resemble a snake's head, and asked Wilson what he would do if he were actually bitten by one of these poisonous species he had been discussing so entertainingly.

"Call for help, I suppose," he answered, "and hope it is you who arrives with the snake bite kit."

Carolyn smiled and Nancy gently brushed his knee with her hand. Howard attempted to launch into an earnest discussion of snake bite treatment, but just as Mrs. Halliday entered with the coffee and cookies, Steven pushed it aside with a comic, belated saying of grace, in which he prayed that their endless bounty of fish might be varied some evening with a meal of snake meat. He praised its delicate flavor and high nutritional value until Joanie got him to admit that he had never tasted it. Neither had any of the rest of them. Nor were there any volunteers when Steven, only half-jokingly, Wilson thought, asked for a show of hands of those willing to participate in a snake hunt, promising that he would gladly do the cooking. While he talked, they rose with their coffee to adjourn to the living room and veranda.

Wilson, still sitting and stirring cream and sugar into his coffee, heard Nancy stand and say to Sarah, across the table, "Why do you suppose we choose to work in these dangerous places?"

"Because," Sarah suggested, "there are no others?"

At the far end of the dining room overlooking the front lawn, Steven and Howard, coffee cups in hand, laughed together, each with a foot propped up on the window seat.

6.

"You're a sad man, Charlie," she said.

He looked out past her through the veranda screens toward the crumbling fountain in the center of the patio. He could just make it out in the fading light, but could no longer see, though he knew they were there, the four stone turtles whose mouths had once spouted water to the four cardinal points of the compass.

"I suppose," he said. He had inspected the fountain by daylight in the first week they'd been there and found the basin so badly cracked it would have been unusable even if the plumbing had been operable, which he doubted. He had been amazed at what good condition they had found most things in when they arrived: the rooms clean and the house only slightly musty; the generator operating to run the lights and water pump and radiophone; the van and all their supplies delivered by barge; the dock repaired and a boat hired for the summer. The staff that the Commission had hired from the mainland to get everything ready for them had been knowledgeable and efficient – not qualities that Wilson had learned he could generally rely on. Now he wanted to make some small physical contribution of his own to the place before the time came to leave, something like getting the fountain working, some small piece of reclamation. Something that would matter.

They sipped their coffee, long since cool, and listened to the sounds of the others from inside the mansion. The insects were so fierce in the evenings that no one went outside, except to work. Now, from the next room, they could hear low voices and the clatter of tiles as the evening Scrabble game got underway, and from further inside someone poking idly at the old Knabe. It was a beautiful piano, Wilson had seen, but so warped now from years uncared for in this humid climate that it was beyond all possibility of restoration. He did not understand how it could have been left there like that. He knew people did that sort of thing all the time, that there was nothing in the world, no matter how valuable, that could not be subject to neglect, but he did not understand it.

"So tell me," she said.

"Tell you?"

"Tell me the sad."

"Oh." He heard her cup click down on the saucer.

"Come on, Charlie," she said, "it's going to be a long summer here and only so many hours of work we can do each day. Are we going to know each other or are we not going to know each other?"

"Give me a break, Nancy," he said. He was stalling for time while he thought about that, even though he knew the answer

37

already. He wanted another cup of coffee, preferably iced, only they weren't making any ice because the ancient freezer frosted up too fast. He even had a mild desire for a drink, but one of the things they had all agreed on was to forego drinking for the summer. No booze. No cigarettes. No dope. Only what mattered: the island, the turtles, the summer, the project. The people. Sometimes he wished he'd had the credentials to sign on for the turtles.

"You tell *me*," he pleaded.

"Listen," she said, "that's no big deal and you know most of it already anyway. I'm just another biochemist looking for what to do. I'm just here for the project, like everyone else. I'm just in for the duration, this year, next year, ten years, whatever it takes I suppose, and in between the summers I will just go back and do my work and live my life. Just meet a few people. Just try to make sure I do things the way I want to do them."

What's all this *just,* Wilson wanted to ask her, but just then something grunted out in the darkness beyond the patio and Nancy turned and said, "Fucking pigs."

"It won't work," he said, but then he realized she'd think he meant it was their solution to the pig problem that wouldn't work. Well, that wouldn't work either, he was convinced. It was totally dark on the screened-in veranda now, but he heard her scrape her chair around toward him. Right this minute there were probably a couple of pigs out there on the beach rooting up turtle eggs. They had worked almost all day every day for the past two weeks stretching barbed wire across the top of the dunes to keep the pigs off the beach, but every morning they found the tracks where the pigs had made their way through and the rooted up, broken, turtle eggs. These were feral pigs, smart and wily; they had practically overrun the island since it had been abandoned, and there seemed no way to contain them, except to introduce a natural predator, some small carnivore that wouldn't be dangerous to humans, a bobcat perhaps. Meanwhile they were waiting for the arrival of a small portable generator they had ordered, to electrify the fence, since the beach was too far from the mansion to be serviced by the main generator. And who knew what the ultimate effects of introducing a predator would be; there was other wildlife on the island as well, wild horses, deer, a multitude of small animals. It was a complex problem. They were, thought Wilson, all complex problems.

She leaned forward in the dark—he could smell her, see the whites of her eyes—and placed her hands on his knees and said, "I know it won't work."

"I didn't mean the pigs," he explained, "I meant the *just.*"

"So did I," she said.

"Well," he said, "you asked about it."

"Go on."

He leaned back in his chair, but as he did so he reached forward and placed one of his hands on top of each of hers where they still rested on his knees. He could feel the pressure of her knees pushed right up against his, too.

"It is just," he said, "just, that there is no just. You can't *just* put a family of bobcats on this island and think that they will *just* do what they are supposed to do and *just* control the pig population. You cannot *just* turn that fountain on out there without starting up a whole chain of activities, some beyond our knowledge and others beyond our ability. You cannot just leave a piano untended in a climate like this without destroying something precious forever, and you cannot turn on just one little flashlight on the beach on the night of the hatch without adding just that one small glimmer to the celestial imprint that just might keep the adult turtles from finding their way back to that beach again, ever. And it may be just one beach, but for them it is the only one."

"This makes you sad?"

"Just," he continued. "*Just* makes me sad. You can't just go home and do your work because you aren't just a worker."

"I know," she said.

"And you can't just come here for the project, either. We aren't just here for the laying and the hatching, we're here all the time between, too, and we aren't just working, either, we're eating and swimming and writing letters home and feeling things and screwing, some of us, for all I know, and sitting out here on the veranda in the dark. Christ, Nancy, you can't *just* sit here on the veranda with me. Do you think those people in there playing Scrabble think we're just sitting here?"

"Charlie," she said, turning her hands over, palms up, to hold his, "we're not just sitting here."

"Shit," he said. He hoped she couldn't see him weeping in the dark. "This isn't *just* an island, either. Whatever this is, it is because of the mainland back there; without that, there wouldn't be any here. This just–just!–reinforces the connections and we can't just go back there in two months as if we'd never been here any more than we can just come here as if . . ."

"Charlie, is there someone back there? Something? That's the sad, isn't it?"

"No," he cried. "Yes. Shit." The pig grunted again far out in the darkness on the lawn beyond the turtle fountain and the patio.

"Oh shit, shit, shit," he said. He lifted his hands from hers and clamped them to his head. "I just wanted to come here and do my work, just like you, but it won't work, don't you see? You can't just have your work and your independence because sooner or later you end up sitting on the veranda in the dark with someone, and you can't just sit with someone because someone isn't just there for you to sit with, and you can't just care for someone, either, because . . . because . . . by and by . . ."

"Go ahead, Charlie, it's OK." She had her hands on his face now, so he knew she could feel how he was weeping and didn't even try to hold it back any longer.

"Because," he wept, "because by and by someone is not sitting with you on the veranda any longer, that is because why. Because by and by you are alone, for all your caring, but you are never just alone, never again just alone. Because wherever you are you are never just there, you are always looking back, at the same time, even in the dark, toward where you have been."

"Gone away?" she asked softly.

"However you want to put it," he shuddered.

"Dead?"

He nodded in her hands. She pressed his face gently between them.

"And you could still care just a little?"

He shrugged. "I would bet against it," he said, not meaning whether or not he could care just a little. "It's too hard. There is no just. Everything's tangled up together and I'm not just here, like I said, even though we also *are* here. I'm sure you're not just here either. It's such a struggle. And even here it's not just us. It won't work, Nancy. If this were a horse race, I would bet everything I have on Won't Work."

They were standing now, but she still held his wet face in her hands, and he knew she was looking straight at him, her height identical to his, her eyes fixed on his even in the total dark of the veranda.

"And yet?" she said.

He tried to smile, even knowing she couldn't see it. "I would bet my whole bundle on Won't Work," he said, "and yet I will be at the rail cheering Will Work all the way to the finish line."

The True Story of How My Grandfather Was Smuggled out of the Old Country in a Pickle Barrel in order to Escape Military Conscription

NATURALLY I WOULD like to help you, especially since I appreciate just having a visitor, especially in the middle of the week, especially such a one as yourself. No one comes in the middle of the week, and even on Sunday it's rare to see such youth and beauty and vitality. They come dragging in here on Sunday half my age and acting twice as old, but who can blame them, the place is not exactly invigorating, is it? Well, you're a kind and sensitive young woman, and also you're family. Time was, not so long ago as you might think, I'd have been wishing you weren't family, if you get what I mean. That's all history now, but it's history you say you've come for, so I will try to cooperate by giving you what I can of it, though to tell you the truth I have been gaining less and less respect for it as time goes on. You would perhaps think that time would give you an increasing admiration for the long view of history as the years pass, but I assure you that isn't so. Maybe just the opposite is true. This is a lesson you could learn much faster if you had come to visit, say, Jake over there in the corner beside the TV. Maybe you will just mosey over there and say Hello to him later on, he doesn't get much in the way of visitors. Then you will see what the long view looks like. It is your misfortune, however, to be afflicted with an aging relative—they are always talking about *aging* around here, though I keep reminding them that we are not aging, we are aged, aged—well, anyway, it is your problem to have to cope with an old man whose mind is still reasonably sharp no matter how many parts of his body are no longer up to doing what they once used to do. The body too becomes history, which is maybe part of the reason for my diminishing respect for it, however much I am aware, thanks to the consolations of television and public radio, that history is a big thing these days, oral history in particular and especially this quest for family history that has blessed me with your presence today.

But what can I tell you? As you know, since it's what you're inquiring about for openers, they have always told a very simple story in our family about how my grandfather was smuggled out of the old country in a pickle barrel in order to escape military conscription. At least I used to think of it as a simple story when I was much younger—when I was a child, a boy, a young man. Now, I am no longer so sure I can help you with it. I heard it several times each year back then, and always it seemed very straightforward and simple: the notice of conscription, panic in the family, offers of assistance, the pickle barrel, night, secrecy, the creaky wagon, the border crossing. . . . But over the many decades since then, numerous changes seem to have crept in. Who knows where they have come from. Now the version I overhear my grandchildren telling their children seems to have little or no relation to the version I heard myself so long ago and, still long ago, passed on to my own children. I cannot believe the events they are speaking of are actually supposed to have happened to my own grandfather. Surely they happened to some stranger instead, in some other country, at some other time. Granted I am a very old man now and have seen a great many changes in my time, more than you would believe. You probably think things have always been the way they are today, but let me tell you, that just isn't so. I won't bore you with the details, which would bore me even worse. The point is that I cannot believe that a simple story that I knew so well in my own younger days—a truly simple story, believe me, with a minimum of characters, few events and those brief and crudely sketched, no real plot to speak of, just that simple – has changed so much within my own lifetime as to become almost completely unrecognizable. Granted, it's been a long lifetime, but a simple story is still a simple story. How much can happen to it, even in the course of ninety some years? A single human lifetime just doesn't seem like time enough for all that to have happened, for a simple story such as the one you want to hear, one that belongs to the family, to have lost its clear outlines and become . . . something else altogether, something that no longer seems to belong to the family at all.

But maybe that's just the way it is with history. A little time goes by, not so much as you'd like to think, and what have you got? It occurs to me that if you took another twenty nonagenarians of my own particular level of achievement – mid-nonagenarians, that is to say, disregarding their mental conditions – and surely there are that many of us in this establishment, with maybe a couple more to spare in case one of us kicks off in the midst of this little experiment – anyway, as I was saying, if you took the twenty of them plus me and lined us up down the long white corridors of history just the way we toddle down the long white corridors here three times a day toward the stink of the dining room, we would stretch all the way back to the birth of Christ. Just think of that, will you: twenty-one nonagenarians, fewer than I could assemble in the courtyard out there in fifteen minutes with a simple tug at the fire alarm, are all you'd need, strung out in sequence, to cover all of human history back to the time of Christ. Not a lot of people when you think about it, is it? Of course, there are some of these old folks, including a few of the ones I've got lined up for you here on our excursion into history, who would get on me pretty quick just for talking about Christ, to say nothing of giving their ages away, but what difference does that make? What do they know about Christ anyway? For that matter, what does anyone know? When you think about what happened to that simple little story about my grand-

44

father in the pickle barrel just in my one single lifetime, think of what must have happened to the story of Christ – which surely, from all I have heard, has got to be a lot more complicated than my grandfather's story – in twenty-one lifetimes. Forget it! The point is, twenty more people like me and bingo, there you are. Toss in another handful and you've got the Golden Age of Athens. A few more and you can start shaking hands with Moses. Makes human history, which we seem to be so awfully proud of, seem like a mighty small thing when you think about it like that, doesn't it? When you realize that the ordinary twenty-five-man roster of your major league baseball club, if it were all made up of players of my own vintage, would have enough combined years to plunge us back into the darkness of prehistory. A minor league club if you prefer, and even a last-place team if you really want to add to the indignity. Throw in the decrepit manager and a couple of wrinkled old coaches as well, and see where you are then. Do you like sports? Of course, a healthy young woman like you. Well, this is a sort of ultimate old-timers' game, made up of my favorite age group, nonagenarians all. They are the visiting team, naturally, what else could they be, and they are all lined up along the third-base line, caps in hand, the few grey strands they own among them waving in the breeze just like the flag while a young soprano, not unlike yourself, stands at home plate singing the national anthem. But only the first few old-timers to her left can hear her, beyond that deafness takes over. Those standing out by third base can hardly see her. They themselves are growing dim to the sight as well, and as the line passes on down the left-field foul line the figures in it soon begin to disappear from view altogether. Out toward the fence, it is impossible to say if anyone is truly there or not. We know they are there, it says so in our programs, but they have taken on the quality of the purely legendary, and who is to say what is really happening out there in the dim and distant past.

No no, I myself was never a professional ball player of any sort, but I am a fairly devoted spectator, even though my spectating is pretty much limited to the TV these days. Well, yes, once or twice a summer, always on the hottest days it seems, they come and take us out to the ball park in a bus, but for all the pleasure of it, it might as well be a journey in a pickle barrel, what with the whining and complaining about the heat, and the air conditioner on the blink, and people wanting to go back to the Home as soon as we've left and not understanding the game and getting sick on the hot dogs and, if you'll excuse me, pissing their pants, too. Frankly, I'm happier to stay here, where I can sit in front of the TV and concentrate on the game itself, at least so long as someone doesn't change the channel. I can watch anything when you get right down to it, not just baseball but any sort of game, basketball, bowling, sailing, ice skating, you name it, because even though I can't remember half an hour later which team or person or horse was the winner, they are all games of numbers, and numbers, as I have been showing you, can be very revealing. The game itself is history the moment it's over, and what can you really know of history? Already on the post-game show they're arguing over what really happened. But the numbers are always with us. Five. Nine. Eleven. One-on-one. Amazing how the odd numbers predominate, as if there is always some sort of imbalance, asymmetry, at work in the world. Yes yes, you can tell me that there are six to a side in hockey, but in fact there are only five real skaters, what is a goaltender but a sort of living gate, and how many times a game, besides, do penalties disrupt the balance of numbers on the ice even more? And think of the random assemblages of track and field teams, of three horses or twenty-three at the post for the Kentucky Derby, of the solitary maniac crossing the Atlantic by plane or sailboat or hot-air balloon. We like to think of games as representatives of the known, as security blankets of order in the chaotic world, as firmly established in time and space, ruled by the fixed perimeters of the out-of-bounds lines, the established confines of the time clock, covered

46

on all sides by rulebooks and referees, by ten frames, three periods, fifteen rounds, and the measured placement of the high hurdles; but the hurdles topple while the runners run on, overtimes pile up on overtimes, crucial plays take place out-of-bounds, the runner stumbles in an open field, the umpire can't decide between safe and out, the piston blows in the last lap, and the giant center stuffs the ball in the wrong basket. Oddity prevails. Anything can happen. The diver catches her toenail on the edge of the board. The jockey's whip catches the wrong horse. The left fielder catches a foul fly and the winning run tags up at third and scores. The two-miler catches the leader on the turn and eases up down the stretch only to realize, as everyone races past him, that there is still another lap to go. The whole team catches the bus to the wrong town. I tell you nothing that hasn't actually happened. It is catch-as-catch-can, as chaotic as the great world itself, and I can have it all for my own convenience right here in front of me on a nineteen-inch diagonal screen. No wonder I am such a devoted spectator.

Of course, as you say, it is "just a game." That is what they've always said, and when did I ever contest such a notion? When did I ever object to the claim that it meant nothing? If anything, I would say that that is precisely the point I have been trying to make, that in spite of every effort that has been made to render the game as something special, something that exists solely within its own confines, which is to say not the confines of ordinary life, the game forever ends up being exactly like life itself, just as odd and unpredictable and chaotic, nothing special, nothing much. Neither chess nor the Olympics can be separated from politics nor baseball from the labor-management struggle nor college sports from educational and ethical issues nor any athlete from the frailties and idiosyncracies of mind and body, from bad weather and financial difficulties and family pressures. So it is just a game then, which isn't much, which is just like life, which is just what goes on.

Which is just my opinion of course, but look around you here and you will discover that what goes on is not the game of balance and order we thought we were watching – or playing – but a considerable mess instead, not unlike our regular Saturday night stew, which has a week-long, indiscernible history of its own. In spite of the fact that you just want to get my grandfather's story straight once and for all, for the record, for the family chronicles, for your high school oral history project – all of which I will do my very best to help you with – I do not think you are too young to understand this. It is not just people who grow senile and sloppy, but the world itself, and all that happpens in it. I can tell you exactly, word for word, the story of my grandfather's flight from the old country to escape military conscription, but look what has happened to it in the meantime. Look at how it has grown old and senile, look how it stumbles and disintegrates, how it comes apart at the seams like an old coat so loose and baggy now that everyone can wear it, though formerly it was a garment of good, sturdy worsted, well-sewn and a precise fit. I suppose it is a good thing, for your sake at least, that I myself have retained throughout the years such a clear and accurate picture of it, true in every detail to the original, though precisely what good that does I'm not at all sure I can say, when we can see how all around us the world is blurring and fading, how even when the brain works the knees don't, and if you will pardon me again, my dear, it takes a catheter to keep the world flowing in anything resembling its accustomed fashion, and history keeps showing up on the discard pile like Jake over there, smelly and forgetful and asleep in front of the TV set, which rambles on without him, as useless as a four of clubs that fits in no one's hand, though he was once, I assure you, a king in his own right.

Yes yes, I know it's my story you want, or my grandfather's, and not Jake's. Bless you, my dear, we should all get what we want, and I promise you I will do the best I can. But you began by saying it was history you wanted and Jake is history. Well, to look at him, I know. Asleep in a chair is not a thing of beauty. Arms dangling,

48

head flopping on his chest, bathrobe open over his knees. And such knees! And the TV flashing and rattling on with its minute-to-minute junk. Not much. And actually it isn't much, is it? Human history, that is. The thing they make such a big deal of, that very thing they have sent you here on an errand for, that thing they write so many dull books about and try so hard to educate us about on educational television, which I do not think is what Jake is not watching over there. *Us* they're going to teach history to, imagine that! Like teaching water how to be wet, if you ask me.

Well, yes, we do watch the educational TV, since you ask, though it's Jake I really want you to watch, as an object lesson in history which I do not think any young person with a genuine concern for the subject can afford to neglect. But the fact is that there is not a whole lot to do here and so the TV set is on most of the time. History snoozes in front of it and some of the rest of us even try to learn something from it at times and not just watch the soaps and the game shows and the sports. We're not beyond learning, you know, even at our advanced ages, some of us anyway, so we watch the educational channel, too. Just the other day I am afraid I had a rather bitter exchange about that with Mrs. K. Not that she watches educational TV or any TV for that matter. Mrs. K. does découpage. She was just passing through the dayroom here the other day, three or four of us were watching a program on the educational channel about micro-organisms, and she stops behind my chair and looks at the set for a minute, then whacks me on the shoulder and says, "What you watch that kinda stuff for? Micro-organisms! What good's that gonna do you?" As if she'd even hung around long enough to know what a micro-organism was!

But she wasn't without effect, all the same. I tell you that woman's got power, even though for my part I'd rather watch game shows than do découpage. Because she no sooner left for her regular Wednesday afternoon découpage class–makes me wonder what she can still be learning about découpage after fifteen years of weekly classes – than one of those old men is hauling himself up to the set in his walker to change the station. And what'd she do but make us all self-conscious about the possibility that we might be acquiring a bit of useless knowledge in addition to passing the time rather pleasantly. You watch a soap opera or a ball game and no one'd ever think of saying to you, "Whattaya watch that for? What good's it gonna do you?" What I would have asked her, if she hadn't been gone so quick – quick for one of us, you understand, she was no sprinter – was, what difference does it make what good's it going to do us? When did anything we ever learned do us much good? Oh, a few practical bits maybe, like how to boil rice or change spark plugs, and the most good that did was saving you a few minutes figuring out how to do it next time. Big deal. But beyond that? I've read a lot of books, still read them, and been a lot of places and known a lot of people, and if someone had ever asked me what good did any of that ever do, I tell you I'd be stumped. Dumb questions always stump me. It's hard to answer a dumb question without giving away the fact that it's a dumb question, you know, and how does that make someone feel, even Mrs. K.? And this one isn't even worth trying to answer because what does "What good did it ever do you?" have to do with anything? I didn't do any of those things, read any of those books, pal around with any of those people, for the good they might do me. I just did them. Of course, they're finally all a part of me, just like the story of my grandfather's flight from the old country, but who's to say whether that's good or bad, that's just me. You take history, though, that's something else. History wants to look at everything you did, at least if you were a king or a general, and say, "What did he do that for?" I've got no respect for that kind of history, which never lets anybody just do anything. That kind of history is Mrs. K. walking through the throne room or field headquarters. But the king and the general, they're just doing, no matter how hard Mrs. K whacks them on the ermine cape or the gold épaulettes.

That kind of history isn't even educational TV, it's just another game show, a kind of big board bingo where if you can find some reasons to connect up a row of events you win the big prize, which is generally just another book on history. But if you really want to know what history is, you should move in here with me for a while. Yes, I know that is not exactly practical and you have got just this one project to do plus school to go back to, but nonetheless I could show you history that way, and it is my personal belief that you would never forget it, it would not be like memorizing names and dates and battles and treaties. Not at all. I would sit you down to lunch with history, though that might not be such a good beginning because you could lose your appetite for history real fast. I could let you talk with history and watch TV with history and even go to découpage class with history. Everybody here is history, and a lot of it, and if you want to understand why I don't think so highly of human history, you should try moving in here and living with it for a while.

Starting maybe with our friend Jake over there, who even seems to be coming awake at the moment. You want history, dear, I'll give you history. Look, did you see an eye open or did you not? Well, perhaps it was only an illusion. Still, that is history sitting there in the person of Jake who routed a whole platoon single-handedly at the Battle of the Marne, Jake who stayed in Paris after the War and hung around with the literati, your Steins and Hemingways and the like, and even published a book himself, though I believe not much came of it. A long narrative poem on dolphins, I think I have been told, or was it porpoises? Anyway, the same Jake who came back home and made it big in land, and I'm telling you big, millions big, and then of course lost it all in the Crash, Jake who considered jumping out of his skyscraper office window but rode the rails instead. Are you getting the picture? Do I have to give you Jake with Oklahoma oil strikes, Jake with a tank command in North Africa in World War II, old grey-headed dropout Jake wandering Haight-Ashbury in the sixties, and Jake bankrolling Clean Gene with the oil money he'd stashed away? I'm not making this up, my little historian, don't have to, this is Jake, the real Jake, Jake-right-over-there-by-the-TV-set, that I'm giving you. But he's only one. I could also give you Hilda, who never leaves her room anymore: Hilda and the Suffragettes, Hilda and the Dustbowl, Hilda teaching Soviet farmers. I could give you Max and the scientific mafia at Göttingen or Arnold and the Spanish Civil War or Henrietta and the Dada movement. Do any of these things mean anything to you? Never mind. Take your pick. This is history we've got right here in this place, the history of the whole twentieth century at least, since most of us were too young before the turn of the century to do much more than go to school or peddle newspapers – though sometimes those newspapers we were selling on street corners told us about things we can still remember, things happening in our own lifetime: the death of Queen Victoria, the Spanish-American War. Jake was a newsboy! Jake was there when Lindy went up and when the Graf Zeppelin came down. Never mind, the particulars don't make any difference, the point is that that's history, that's Jake, Jake is history.

And what does it all add up to? Just stay to dinner tonight and I'll serve you history. Forget about moving in, I don't think you're ready for that yet, but a single meal maybe you could handle. Sit down at the table with us tonight – late this afternoon, actually, they feed us early here in the hopes that they can get some food down us to keep us alive before we fall asleep, unfed, forever, though it doesn't always work. Anyway, stay to dinner and you'll get history à la carte. History that has to be wheeled in to the table. History that has to be spoonfed its mashed this and creamed that. History that pees in its pants in the middle of the dining room and weeps in its chopped steak and drools its applesauce till it's time to get wheeled away again.

That's what history adds up to, finally, and like I told you, it isn't much, is it? Stay around and see for yourself, if you really think you have a stomach for history. And then I will tell you the simple little story of how my grandfather fled the old country in a pickle barrel in order to escape military conscription. Which isn't exactly history, you understand, but just a little family text learned by rote long, long ago; a recitation no one ever much listened to anyway, like a poem memorized at school; today, who knows, perhaps as many versions as there are tellers; a report from the front disintegrating in the messenger's pocket even as he gallops through the rain to deliver it. Whereas here you will be getting a first-class chance to see the real thing, history as it is, without having to wait till you get like Jake yourself, because you're history too, remember, just like Jake, just like me and my grandfather, and in all probability, much as it may dismay you to hear it now, you will also end up just like this, no matter how much you sit there shaking your lovely curls, just like Jake, yes, just like history, which is not entirely without its blessings, however, since history doesn't know it's history, fortunately, and Jake is in such a condition that he doesn't know what condition he's in. Some blessing, huh? If Jake knew what his condition was, do you know what he'd do? Precisely, the same thing you or I would do under the circumstances. The thing is, though, that if Jake knew what his condition was, then Jake wouldn't be in that condition and wouldn't have any reason to do what he would naturally do if he knew he was in that condition. A lot of good self-knowledge does, huh?

And what's history, after all, but the big picture in the quest for self-knowledge, the attempt to know our condition as a nation or a culture or worse yet some god-forsaken ethnic group, as if that sort of knowledge was likely to do us any more good than the individual kind. What you can say of Jake you can believe writ large as well. If the British had known what their condition was vis-à-vis the colonies in the seventeen-seventies, believe me, they wouldn't have been in that condition, they'd have found some other way of dealing with their new-world imperialism. Ditto the Rome of the decline and fall. The Jews in their Exodus. Imperial America in Vietnam. Neanderthal man. Modern woman. Probably even God, who with some knowledge of the divine condition would no longer be God but God's God. That's the heart of the condition, you know – yours, mine, Jake's, history's, God's – that it's always just eluding us. Simply by acknowledging that you live in a condition of ignorance you show enough knowledge to no longer be living in the condition of ignorance. Claim to be living in a state of knowledge, though, and bingo, the minute you make such an ignorant statement, the state of knowledge leaps away from you and there you are right back in the condition of ignorance again. Unknowingly, of course. Might as well have said screw self-knowledge and stayed there in the first place.

Well, I know you are here on a grand educational mission, part of which is to understand your own condition by understanding your ancestors, but when you look at it like that, it makes you wonder, doesn't it? Is it the essence of our condition, always, not to know what our condition is? Never mind, I wasn't looking for an answer, I wouldn't even know how to begin to test the validity of such a statement. If we were to accept it, however, just take it on faith maybe, it could save us all a lot of time and effort chasing our own tails, which is maybe just what history is, after all, humanity chasing its own tail, too busy looking over its shoulder at what it's attached to, where it's been, to see where it is and where it's going. Is that the way it works? I have had a lot of dogs in my lifetime, from childhood right up through the final years before they put me in here. They don't allow pets in here, you know, might confuse them with the residents. I had big dogs and little dogs, inside dogs and outside dogs, purebreds and mongrels, and I never saw a single one, beyond its puppyhood, chase its own tail. If my experience holds true for the species, maybe it proves that dogs are even smarter than we give them credit for, and quite sensibly free from our own obsession with self-knowledge. I suspect that the puppy that chases its own tail is doing so precisely because it doesn't know it's its own tail, and that once it grows up enough to recognize that that thing back there is just its own tail, then it's free to ignore it and just go on and do its doggie business, which ought to be enough for anyone, if you ask me.

But listen, that's the dinner bell now. You don't have to rush off, you know, my invitation still holds, we have dinner guests regularly, it's no trouble at all for the kitchen, you'd be appalled to see how much food gets wasted here. Well, perhaps another time. But listen, don't hurry, it takes this gang a long time to totter and wheel themselves down to the dining room, we've got plenty of time. If you'll just sit back down here with me for a few minutes more, I will tell you the true story of how my grandfather was smuggled out of the old country in a pickle barrel in order to escape military conscription.

The Man in the Cardboard Mask

LEONARD, WHO HAD been having a lot of trouble with his face lately, was having lunch with his friend Nathan Grip at the Athletic Club after their racquetball game. Leonard admired Nathan as one of those natural people who looked comfortable, right in place, whatever he was doing, such as slouching now with his leg draped over the arm of the chair and holding a cup of coffee in one hand and the saucer in the other. Nathan was easy and graceful on the racquetball court, too. So much so, in fact, that it always surprised Leonard, who felt stiff and awkward in any game he played, even chess or working a crossword puzzle, to realize how often he won their matches. Whether it was on the racquetball court, like today, or outside on the tennis court in nicer weather, Leonard, watching Nathan's perfect form and graceful moves, always felt as if he himself had been assembled from an Erector set. Yet he almost always won their matches, and it was only because he had a predictable let-down in the second set or game, a loss of motivation, that the final score usually came out 2–1 in his favor, as it did today, instead of 3–0. He was sure this had to bother Nathan – it would certainly have bothered *him* to have such grace count for nothing – but it wasn't a subject he could discuss with Nathan, who was a client as well as a friend. He felt certain it would come out sounding as if he were rubbing it in, when in fact he only wanted to apologize. But maybe, he reasoned, Nathan even had enough grace to be comfortable with the failures of grace.

For his own part, Leonard had never felt further removed from grace. He couldn't recall just when the trouble with his face had begun or how it had grown to its present proportions. Somehow it had just developed, without his really noticing it, until now, when he laughed, it felt as if it wasn't his own face at all but some stiff, ugly thing that he was being forced to wear. After forty years of living with it, he thought a face should be comfortable, but instead his felt like cardboard when he laughed.

When he tried to hide this feeling, things got even worse. He would try to suppress the laugh before the cardboard face took over, but he could never quite manage to do it in time. He enjoyed his life and liked to laugh, but now his laugh, which was the kind that people called infectious and joined in on, had become like a little hand that reached out of his open mouth and grabbed hold of the cardboard mask and pulled it up over his face. First he could sense it closing in around his lower jaw, then tightening about his chin, then creeping up over his lips. Leonard tried to combat this both by holding back on his laugh, which was impossible to do once his famous infectiousness set in, and by pulling another, opposing mask down over his face. This was a mask of solemnity, and Leonard would will it to start from his hairline and descend over his forehead and enclose his dark eyes and heavy nose and eventually to push the cardboard mask back from the beachhead it had established on his tightening upper lip. The problem was that even when he succeeded in driving the cardboard mask back off his face altogether, Leonard ended up feeling as if he were still wearing a mask and not his own familiar face. This other mask seemed to him to be made of some very cool and shiny metal, like aluminum. And when he suddenly stopped laughing and people looked at him, still laughing themselves, to see what was the matter, he was sure that they could tell at once that he was wearing a face that was not his own, an inhuman, metal face.

He had come to think of the aluminum face as Smith, which

was his name but wasn't really his name. Leonard's parents were named Smith and he had aunts and uncles and many, many cousins who were also named Smith; his paternal grandparents, both of them only recently deceased, were Smiths, and on his dresser he had a restored photograph of his great-grandfather Smith. Leonard's real name, however – the whole family's real name, as everyone in the family knew – was Cohen. Leonard had known this since he was a child. It had become a family tradition to explain to each child, before it was sent off to begin school, that its real name was not Smith but Cohen, and Leonard had explained this fact to his own children, who were very precocious, almost as soon as they began to talk. As a child himself, Leonard had never been quite comfortable knowing that he was called one thing, that it said Smith, Leonard, in his teacher's roll book, but that his real name was something else, and often on the playground when other children called him Smitty, it took him a moment to respond, to realize who they were calling. He was never embarrassed or even confused by this, just uncomfortable; by junior high he had everyone calling him Lenny, and later it became just Len and now no one except fairly crass new acquaintances who were trying to rush the friendship ever called him Smitty.

It was because of Leonard's great-great-grandfather that the family was called Smith and not Cohen, and it had nothing to do with that patriarch's being ashamed of being Jewish or embarrassed at having so blatantly Jewish a surname. It was just that when this founding father of the family arrived in America, already very old and speaking no English at all, it seemed to him that everybody he met in America was already named Cohen and so, since they had come here to make a new start after all, he decided that his family should have a new name to accompany this new start in the new world. Smith had sounded good to him: it was different; he had never known anyone by that name before.

Leonard and everyone else in the family knew this story of

Great-great-grandfather Cohen-Smith's decision by heart, having heard it, and told it themselves, from early childhood on; everyone who married into the family came to know the story equally well, and so did the families of those who married out of the family, and so changed their names and were no longer either Smiths or Cohens, in most cases. In one case, that of Leonard's beautiful Aunt Katie, who was not much older than he was, a Smith had gone off to Radcliffe to college and ended up marrying another Smith, a real Smith, from Harvard. In several other cases Smith women had married Cohens and had thereby acquired their real names as no Smith man could. Leonard also knew from childhood stories that in every generation there had been a zealot who had campaigned endlessly to get the family to take legal action to restore its real name. In Leonard's own generation the zealot was his cousin Ralph, who owned Cohen's Deli, a name which Ralph had inherited from its previous proprietor. Leonard had been in the deli often and had heard how all the old customers addressed Ralph, standing behind the counter in his white apron, as "Mr. Cohen," so he could understand Ralph's personal interest in the matter. But Leonard thought that at this late date – with the family well into its fifth generation of Smith and he himself entering his fifth decade – such a change would be totally silly, no matter how uncomfortable anyone felt with the current state of things.

Leonard's ex-wife Marjorie knew even better than he did what it was like to go from a Cohen to a Smith. She had been a Cohen herself, not a Smith-Cohen but a real Cohen, her father a rabbi, the rabbi who married them, in fact, and to whose congregation they had belonged until the end of their marriage. Rabbi Cohen was a smiling, good-hearted man who liked everybody and probably wouldn't have objected even if his only daughter had married outside the faith, but Marjorie always resented being a Smith. They were the only Smiths in the congregation – the rest of Leonard's family belonged elsewhere – and it always made her feel vaguely out of place, as if she—the rabbi's daughter!—were a convert. It embarrassed her, she complained that it made her feel as if she were trying to pass as Jewish, and every time Leonard sat down with the children to explain about the name, she got up and stalked out of the room. As soon as they were divorced she became Marjorie Cohen again.

Leonard, of course, was still Smith, and his old friend Nathan, who knew the whole story of the Smith family name, was sipping his coffee now in the Athletic Club dining room and telling a joke about a man named Cohen. Nathan often told Leonard Jewish jokes, and Leonard, leaning forward against the table with his hands in his lap, knew this was only because Nathan liked to have fun giving him a hard time. The Athletic Club had only recently begun to accept Jewish members, and Leonard, filling out the application form with the name Smith, had realized for the first time, though in a reverse sort of way, what Marjorie had felt when she complained about passing: now that the Athletic Club would finally accept Cohens, he was joining as a Smith. Not that there was ever any question about his getting into the Club: applications had to be presented by a current member, and he had the support of Nathan Grip, whose family had been charter members.

Now Nathan delivered the punch line of his joke, breaking up into laughter, loud laughter, so that heads turned at other tables in the dining room and he even had to set his cup and saucer down on the table in order to avoid spilling his coffee. And Leonard was laughing, too, not just to prove that he was a good sport and could take a racist joke, but also because he found it genuinely funny. He wanted to respond by telling Nathan the Wasp variation on the same joke, which one of the fellows in his office had told him only yesterday. In the Wasp version the victim's name had been Smith, though Leonard's colleague, in embarrassment, had changed it to Wilson halfway through the telling. He was tempted to repeat it now for Nathan's benefit, but because he could feel his face turning to cardboard already, he decided to change the subject. He asked Nathan about his children. Nathan, who had just settled down enough to begin to sip his coffee again, burst into laughter once more, sprayed a mouthful of coffee over the table, waved it away as if such a mess were the most natural thing in the world, and explained to Leonard, between further fits of laughter, that his ex-wife, who was about to marry an English banker, had been after him to agree to changing the children's names to her new husband's name, which was Smith.

Leonard, his whole face a crinkled sheet of cardboard now, laughed along with him.

"I suppose that's only fair," he said, "since Marjorie's still lobbying to change our kids from Smith to Cohen."

Four years after the divorce, Leonard still saw Marjorie frequently, though he told no one except his girlfriend about this. It was an easy secret to keep because Marjorie didn't want anyone to know about it either. She wouldn't invite him into her house because she didn't want the children getting ideas, and when the children were away at camp during the summer, she didn't want the neighbors getting ideas. The neighbors knew her parents. For the same reasons, she didn't want to be seen with him in public, so they couldn't go to movies or parties or concerts or restaurants. She had even cajoled him into resigning his membership in her father's congregation because she didn't want to deal with the problems of who would sit where during the holidays and what would people think if they saw them walking and talking together after services. Like all her other decisions about how they would continue to see each other, she made this one by herself and then explained it to Leonard very carefully. He had readily agreed to rejoin the congregation his own family had always belonged to; it didn't make a lot of difference to him, since he only attended services on the High Holy Days, and not always then.

So the only place they ever saw each other was at his apartment. Today he had come back to his office after lunch with Nathan to find a note on his desk saying that his ex-wife had called and would be bringing one of the children over in the evening. Later, however, when he buzzed her in, and stood in the open doorway watching her get off the elevator and walk down the hall, he could see that she was alone.

As soon as she was inside the apartment and he had shut the door, she kicked off her shoes and said, "What was I supposed to tell your secretary, that I wanted to fuck your brains out?"

Sometimes the messages said that she needed him to sign some papers, that she needed help with her taxes, that she would be bringing over a wonderful new book or a pot of soup. His secretary told him how nice she thought it was that he and his ex-wife maintained such a good relationship. He thought it was good, too, but also a little suspect, in ways he could never quite put his finger on. It just seemed like an odd way for two divorced people to be carrying on. Still, he reasoned, no one in the whole world knew him better than Marjorie did, and that mattered to him a great deal. So did the fact that their lovemaking was always terrific. He had gone out with a number of women since the divorce, and though he felt that many of them had more shapely bodies than Marjorie's, with none of them had his lovemaking ever been as wonderful as it continued to be with Marjorie. When he told her, usually with considerable enthusiasm, how he felt about their lovemaking, she always said, "Ummm, me, too," but in a matter-of-fact tone, as if it were obvious and not noteworthy.

Still, there was always a quality of the erratic about the way they got together, as if there was something at the center of the relationship that they couldn't figure out, couldn't explain to each other. Sometimes they would find excuses to see each other three times in a week, sometimes three weeks would go by without their even speaking to each other on the telephone. Sometimes she would call on a Sunday afternoon to say she was coming and bring-

62

ing dinner with her, and then she would arrive empty-handed. Sometimes, when Leonard got excited about some new dish he had just learned to cook and called to invite her over for dinner, she would arrive at his door with her hands full of white cardboard cartons from the Chinese restaurant down the street. Sometimes he would call her at work and they would make plans to meet on their way home, but she wouldn't show up. He never knew whether to feel hurt and angry or to be understanding about her complicated life. Since it was all so puzzling, he was sure that it was best to keep things a secret.

They didn't keep secrets from each other, though, so it was natural for him to talk to her, finally, tonight, about the strange and disturbing feelings he was having about his face.

"You dumb shit," she said, "can't you see you're having an identity crisis?"

She swore like a rabbi's daughter, in English. She was also much quicker in her perceptions than he was, and he knew that and was often overwhelmed by the speed with which she could slash open any statement, perform a skilled autopsy, and pronounce her results while the body was still warm. She spoke with such authority that he always felt he had to accept her analysis as correct and final, though frequently later on, after she had left, or even days later, he would realize that she had been wrong. At the time, however, her decisiveness usually reduced him to silence or agreement or, at the most, mildly expressed doubt.

"I'll think about it," he said this time, though he already felt fairly certain he knew precisely what his identity was. He was a divorced insurance agent going on forty-one years old with two children, the wrong name, and a face that turned to cardboard when he laughed and aluminum when he made it stop laughing.

After she left, he got up and showered and dressed, though it was late, and thought about it. What he thought, finally, was that so far as he could tell he did not have an identity crisis. He had a face crisis.

And maybe, he also thought, I have a laugh crisis. After all, wasn't that the only time his face felt like cardboard, when he laughed? And if he didn't have to cope with the cardboard laugh face, then he wouldn't have the aluminum cover-up face to cope with either. He had poured himself a small brandy and was watching the late night talk show on TV while he thought about this. When the famous comic who was serving as guest host for the evening told the same ethnic joke that Nathan had told Leonard at the Athletic Club earlier in the day, only changing the victim from Jewish to Scandinavian, Leonard felt that the joke lost a lot of its punch. It was still basically a good joke, Leonard thought, but Scandinavians just weren't that funny, so instead of laughing at it this time, he only smiled a little. As his mouth curled up at the edges, his whole face, starting around the cheeks especially, began to feel like cardboard.

Though the feeling went away quickly, the experience frightened him, and he got up at once and turned off the TV. Maybe, he thought, it's getting worse. First with a laugh, then a smile, then maybe when I'm just feeling happy, then all the time.

He went to the window and looked down into the street, which was nearly empty, and wondered what it meant. He heard people talking these days as if every little twitch the body made—every headache, stiff neck, muscle spasm and inflammation—was a secret message from some much more knowledgeable inner self.

"I wonder what my body is trying to tell me," they said.

Leonard heard them listen to their bodies and answer themselves. If their chests pained them, they said it meant they should slow down, though they seldom did so. If it was their lungs or muscles, the body was telling them they needed exercise, and they joined tennis clubs or at least bought new warm-up suits and running shoes. If it was the stomach, then they should change their jobs or their diets, or get divorced. Leonard had always exercised and eaten properly; he liked his job and it was Marjorie who had gotten the divorce, not him. Still, what could it hurt to give this approach a chance?

"What is my body trying to tell me?" he asked himself, still standing in front of the window, smiling a little at the thought of carrying on a conversation like this with his own body, feeling his face beginning to feel like cardboard as he stood there smiling. Down below in the street an occasional car rushed by, headlights on, occupants hidden to his view. His face felt like cardboard all the way up to the eyes. Maybe, he thought, my body is only trying to tell me that my face is turning to cardboard.

He decided to call Elaine, who was the only person he had told about his still seeing Marjorie, a secret he had entrusted to her because he thought it was important to their relationship, his and Elaine's, that she know. He had never dared to tell her about his face, however. They had been going together for nearly six months, but he didn't feel he knew her well enough to predict what her reaction might be. What if she thought he was going crazy? More likely, he expected, she would want him to see a doctor, not a psychiatrist, just a doctor, that was her kind of common-sense approach. He did not feel as if he needed either a psychiatrist or a physician; on the whole he was feeling perfectly fine, but he did, suddenly, feel the need to talk to Elaine about this. They had a date for Friday night, but they were going to a concert, and besides, he didn't want to wait till then to talk with her. He went into the kitchen and dialed her number, only realizing as she answered how late it was and that he had woken her up.

"Why do you always call me after your wife leaves?" she said.

"She's not my wife."

Elaine hadn't objected when he told her that he was still seeing his ex-wife occasionally.

"It's okay," she had said, "I understand, you two have still got a lot of stuff to work out."

They let it go at that; she didn't push him on what "seeing" Marjorie meant or how often "occasionally" was. He thought that one reason she was so fair about this was that she was still dating a couple of other men herself. He wasn't sure how he felt about that, but whatever the reason for her acceptance of his relationship with Marjorie, he was relieved to have it.

Now she just humphed at him over the phone while he tried to figure out how she could possibly have known that Marjorie had been with him that evening. After they had talked for a little while about other things, Leonard finally worked up the courage to say that he would like to see her.

"Right now, Leonard?" He didn't say anything.

"Leonard, I'm sleeping. Or at least I was until you called."

"Listen, Elaine," he finally said, "I have to talk to you. I need your help. I need you to look at me and tell me what you see."

"I look at you all the time, Leonard."

"No, I mean look at my face. Look at my face and tell me what you see."

"I know what your face looks like, Leonard. I can see it as well as if you were here. Better. I don't have any lights on."

He hesitated. "And?"

"You look so young," she said. "You have such a young face."

When he had been quiet for some time, she asked him what he was thinking. He still didn't respond. Actually, what he was thinking was that it was her face, with its smooth pale skin and wide green eyes, that was really young; his own only looked that way because he was using it so little. Finally he thanked her and told her how kind and patient she had been with him and how much he missed her, truly meaning it all, and soon they said goodnight and hung up without talking any more about his face. Her voice had become so soft and sweet when she told him how she saw his face that he actually went to bed feeling a little better about it.

Still, it nagged at him when he got up in the morning that he couldn't feel free to laugh like other people, or even smile now, so

66

he switched his clock-radio off as soon as it woke him because the two broadcasters on his favorite early morning show always told jokes. They were dumb jokes, usually, but the kind that could always get a laugh out of him in the morning. And once a week, today being the day, they did a "worst jokes of the week" routine, which consisted of truly terrible jokes sent in by listeners and always left him smiling for hours afterwards. He did not want to go out into the world this morning feeling all smiley and cardboard.

At first what had mostly bothered him was the fear that other people, especially his clients, would see how his face was stiffening and turning to cardboard. Leonard had always enjoyed his work and his clients, whom he often got to know well and generally thought of as nice people. He liked having a good time with them, meeting with them at their homes or businesses, learning about their families and their interests, and his pleasure in working with them showed. People frequently told him that that was what accounted for his being so successful: people trusted a man who so clearly enjoyed his work. People complimented him on his smile, too. He had perfect, straight teeth, thanks to his parents' belief in the social necessity of orthodonture, but even as a child he was always being told what a lovely smile he had. Once, after his grandmother had said to him, "What a nice smile you have," he had gone immediately into the bathroom and looked in the mirror to see what was so nice about it, but he couldn't find anything special. He assumed that there was something his grandmother and other adults must know that he just didn't know yet, and so went on smiling his smile and not thinking much about it after that.

But now he felt far too self-conscious to go out into the world risking that smile and the cardboard feeling that accompanied it or the equally disturbing feeling of having to pull down his aluminum mask to hide it. Now, in fact, he did not even want to sit at his own breakfast table, alone, feeling like that. It wasn't just a matter of what other people might see, it was a matter of how it felt to him.

Cardboard felt stiff, awful, and aluminum felt worse, impenetrable. Both felt terrible. It felt terrible to smile and terrible to shut down the smile.

He sipped at his coffee, but his whole face felt so stiff he couldn't seem to hold his lips right, and some of the coffee dribbled out of the corners of his mouth and down his chin. When he tried to eat his English muffin, it seemed to be all crumbs. After awhile he got up from the table and went into the bathroom to shave, but his whole face, as he passed the razor over it, felt as if it had been injected with novocaine. He could hear the scrape, scrape of the razor but he couldn't feel anything, as if he were shaving another layer of something that had crept between his face and the razor. He washed his face when he was done shaving, and it looked fresh and clean though he couldn't for the life of him tell whether it had been hot or cold water that he had splashed on it. When he was finished dressing, he called his secretary to say that he wasn't coming into the office this morning, that he was going directly to call on some clients instead.

"What's up, Len?" she asked.

They had been working together for almost ten years and knew each other's moods and intonations better than most married couples, though Shirley was the only one who ever spoke up about these things. Leonard's choice, when he saw that something was bothering her, was to take her out to lunch or bring her some small token, a new coffee cup or even fresh flowers, to cheer her up, or to suggest that she take the afternoon off, which she sometimes did. When she showed concern for him, he usually responded by saying, "Oh, it's nothing" or "I'll be okay" or just shrugging it off.

Today he said, "What makes you ask?"

"I'm not sure," she said, "you just sound a little odd. Sort of stiff."

Leonard said nothing at all.

"Also, your ex-wife called. She left a message. Do you want me to read it to you? Here it is: According to Jung the incomplete is always perceived as inhuman; try to be born. That's what she said: Try to be born. Is that Carl Jung she's talking about? I read Jung and I don't remember that."

Leonard just stared at the receiver, thinking. So Marjorie had gone home last night and diagnosed his facial complaint and called in, first thing in the morning, with a prescription. At least she hadn't arrived at his door with an armload of books, saying, "Here, read these, it's all in here," as she had on past occasions. No, this time she had summarized it, encapsulated it; like a good doctor she had spared him the entire medical school education and boiled it down to a simple treatment, on the level of take-two-aspirins-and-go-to-bed. Try to be born. Maybe not quite so simple. Also, he knew, probably wrong: perceptions as fast as Marjorie's usually struck like lightning, obliterating the data, the logical processes, leaving a charred clearing illuminated by one burning stump of perception, often smouldering so heavily that the whole area was soon hidden under a thick cloud of smoke and it was hard to remember precisely what one had once seen there. It was a great act to watch, until you tried to figure out what it was all about. Besides, if anything like that had been in Jung, Shirley would have known and confirmed it. Shirley was the most thorough and meticulous reader Leonard had ever known, whether she was reading a nineteenth-century novel or the fine print of an elaborate liability policy. She was a master of the written text, never missed a thing, and Leonard had regularly praised her for her precision and accuracy. If it had been Jung, Shirley, who had ploughed through all the saints of psychology in recent years, would surely have known. Still, Leonard thought, just because it was not in Jung does not necessarily mean it was wrong. Wasn't misinterpretation also a route to knowledge? Couldn't it be possible to get Jung wrong and something – something else – right? Or am I, Leonard wondered, still just trying, after all these years, to credit her instant perceptions because I myself have nothing to offer?

Leonard looked at the phone in his hand. He didn't worry about Shirley, who he knew would be keeping her own receiver tucked into her shoulder and waiting for whatever more he had to say while she went on ahead, in the meantime, with her own work. So he kept on looking at the phone as if it were some sort of thing through which he might, finally, expect some sort of illumination, if only he stared at it long enough. But it wasn't, he knew, it was just a thing, and what could you expect from a thing? That, he realized, was what really nagged at him about Marjorie's message, that implication that he, too, was just a thing. Who's inhuman, he wanted to know? Don't I have a headache this morning? Do *things* have headaches? It's not like I'm cardboard all the way through, he told himself. Just a little surface layer. Just now and then. But it did occur to him at once that he might be regressing, that once he was human like everyone else, a complete human male with a face that was also human, a flesh and blood face that was now being replaced by a face that was dry and bloodless, a face of paper or metal, he could have his choice of either but it did not seem he could choose the old flesh and blood model any longer. He didn't know whether he was going back down the evolutionary ladder or on up it, but he did suddenly understand something: things were changing, maybe it was him, maybe it was the world around him, but it, whatever it was, was changing, that was sure.

As he could see it, there were three possibilities. One, the world was getting stranger all the time – he was not unaware that in recent years the word *weird* had gained unprecedented usage on all levels of society – and whatever was happening to him was happening in reaction to this sudden increase in the weirdness of the world. Two, the world was not actually changing, but his perceptions were becoming more acute, so that each time he looked, he saw more clearly how strange the world was and reacted to that fresh intensity of perception by hiding behind cardboard or aluminum every time he deluded himself into thinking the world was something to laugh at. Or, three, actually it was only he who was becoming stranger all the time, just as he had been suspecting, and anything weird he thought he saw in the world was only his own reflection.

There was one other possibility that occurred to him, which, however, he preferred not to consider seriously: namely, four, that he was deluded, and nothing was changing. The text of the world was precise and fixed forever, rigid as an insurance policy signed and notarized by all parties, right down to the tiniest print. If the ultimate particles of matter were decaying, as he'd recently read in a science article in the Sunday Supplement, that wasn't change, that was just a given of the original text, that the ultimate particles would decay. He didn't want to consider this, however, because he felt certain – call it faith, call it stupidity, he didn't care – that *something* was changing, either in himself or in the world. It didn't make much difference which, actually, since he and the world were both part of the same interlocking system. The system was changing. Not for the better, so far as he could tell. Or his perception of the system was changing. That was all the same, too, since his perception was also part of the system. Confusing, that was what he decided it was: the system was changing in the direction of confusion.

He was not thrilled to understand this change, but maybe, he thought, that's not it at all, and I am just confused. Which led him to think of a fifth possibility, namely that it was impossible to know any of the above, it was only possible to accept. To take the world at – good grief, he thought in an aside to himself, am I really saying this? – face value. As it was. The way Elaine seemed to take him. If he was cardboard and aluminum as well as flesh and blood, then he was cardboard and aluminum as well as flesh and blood. Maybe a little glass and plastic and stainless steel, too. Eventually, if not just now.

But what about the other part of the message? Was that something he was being born into or something he should try to be born out of? What was he to do? He looked at the telephone in his hand as if he still had some hope that it might come through with an oracular answer for him.

"Try to be born," he mumbled into it, finally, but that was what the telephone had already said to him, and he could hardly expect any response to his echo. Try asking it a question, he thought.

"Shirley," he said, "what do you think I should do?"

"Hey," she said, "why don't you take the afternoon off?"

Actually, he had been thinking about taking the whole day off. It was a beautiful sunny day. He could go to the museum and the zoo and to lunch all by himself. He never ate lunch by himself. Lunch was always for clients during the week and for family on the weekend: his children on Saturday and his parents on Sunday. He could find some out-of-the-way diner where he'd be sure not to run into anyone he knew. And maybe go to a movie matinee. Maybe a movie in the evening, too. A whole day with pictures and animals and strangers. That was something he could accept right now, without confusion. No one to smile at and no one not to smile at. His face could be completely at ease, it could have a chance to find out what it really was and maybe he could just accept that then and all this nonsense would go away and things would neither be nor seem so strange any longer and neither would he and there would be no more masks rising and descending, no cardboard and aluminum containers for his face, and he could just be himself again, Leonard Smith. If not "again," he thought, then "finally."

"Just me," he said aloud as he patted the telephone where he'd laid it back in its cradle. "Leonard," he said, crossing the living room to look out the window, "Smith."

That wasn't totally him, of course, as he well knew, because that wasn't all there was to his name, and, besides, he also knew that nothing was likely to be quite that simple anyway, because here he was sitting around his apartment all by himself, no one to smile at, no one not to smile at, and still having trouble with his face. A day off was OK, but he also knew it was just an evasion, that it would not in itself solve anything even if it did give him a little break from cardboard and aluminum, that tomorrow he would go back to work, tomorrow he would smile at a client, tomorrow cardboard and aluminum would once again lay claim to his face. And could he just accept that? For what it was? That was the problem, as far as he could tell: he still didn't quite *know* what it was, that face of his. Except cardboard. Or aluminum.

He stood in his living room window looking down at the traffic jam that clogged the street below him, a mass of cars, steel shells in which, from this distance, this angle, he could only presume there were drivers, passengers, people. The sidewalk across the street, though, was crowded with human activity: people walking dogs, carrying parcels, hurrying along or strolling by in no great hurry at all. He couldn't see the sidewalk directly below his window, but he knew that if he could stick his head out and look down he would see people going by in odd perspective: the tops of many heads, heads hatted and hatless, kerchiefed heads, bald heads, wigged heads, dark curls, long hair twisted in the wind. This is all too much, he was thinking, I only want my own face back, but he could no longer remember what his own face felt like. Not what it would feel like to the touch, to his own fingers or Elaine's, but just what it *felt* like, what it felt like all by itself, what it felt like to have his own face and not to feel cardboard or aluminum in its place. Try as hard as he might, he couldn't remember what his face felt like, and this truly alarmed him so that he turned away from the window and went and sat on the couch and put his face in his hands. For a moment he felt quieted, as if his hands were helping him remember the face he must have once had–though he couldn't remember when that might have been, when his face hadn't felt like some alien, cardboard thing–until suddenly he recalled a story he had read in college about a man who had put his face in his hands and then pulled his head back only to discover that his face was still lying there in his hands. Horrified, Leonard stood up, wiped his hands on his pants, and hurried to the front door. The little mirror in the front hall showed him that he was still wearing a face that looked just like his own, but mirrors lie, he thought, they're just like other people, they help us to make up our faces, I've got to get out of here.

But at the zoo, where he went first because it was early and very few people would be around yet, and also because he wanted to be outside, to see what effect fresh air and sunshine might have on his face, things were no better. He chose to visit the big cats first, because of all the animals they had always seemed to him to be the ones most at ease with their own bodies. They were lounging about on the grass in the morning sunshine in their open-air exhibits. It pleased Leonard, as he always told the children when he brought them here, that there were no bars anymore, that things could look so natural. The big male lion rolled over on his back and lay belly-up in the sun. One after another the three huge tigers undulated about the perimeter of their pit. The dozing leopard seemed to flow up onto its four feet, stretched mightily, then slowly subsided into sleep again. But when the leopard woke again a few minutes later and opened its yellow eyes and turned its gaze upon him, Leonard had the distinct impression that the creature was wearing a leopard mask, complete with leopard indolence and wide leopard yawn. And likewise the lion, when Leonard went back to see it, rolled over twice with the playful grace of Nathan Grip casually diving for a backhand shot on the tennis court, and ended up on its side, legs outstretched, looking up out of its pit with what Leonard could clearly see was a lion mask on its face, complete with golden, fluffed-out lion mane. Leonard chose not to look at the tigers again, but as he cut across the far side of the zoo to get back to the parking lot, he couldn't help seeing the chimp clinging to the bars of its old-fashioned cage and grimacing at him through its chimpanzee mask.

In the parking lot Leonard took one look at his shiny new Fiat sitting smugly behind the mask of its Fiat grill and hood and decided to take the bus. When he got to the corner, however, and saw the big red bus bearing down on him with its mouth full of chrome and its tinted front windows opaque in the sunlight, he turned his back to it and started walking. Walking at least freed him from the streets and sidewalks so he could make his own path across the park that surrounded the zoo. And in the park, thank goodness, the grass was just grass and not artificial turf, such as they had at the stadium now, though in a certain sense, Leonard realized, there was even something artificial about the real grass. This was the city, after all, glass and steel and concrete. What was it doing hiding behind this façade of grass? But wasn't everything hiding behind something else, even if, as with the big cats, that something was just itself? On the opposite side of the open space of park he was now crossing stood an old-fashioned-looking gazebo, which Leonard knew, from his previous visits with the children, housed the public toilets. He had a strong urge to call up Nathan Grip, a smart human being who always seemed to know who he was and what he was doing, and ask him what he was concealing behind his particular façade of elegant grace, but there was no phone booth in sight. Probably, thought Leonard, there was one right in front of him, only looking like something else, perhaps that portable toilet a workman was just emerging from on the construction site across the street from the park.

Actually, he had a much stronger urge to call Elaine – no, not to call her, to see her. But by the time he got back to his car he realized that he couldn't do that, that you just don't barge in unannounced on someone in the middle of the morning, especially someone whose home is also her place of work. Besides, he knew how hard she had been working lately to complete the two large oils that Nathan's company had commissioned. That had happened just about the first time they had started going out, she hadn't even met Nathan yet, wasn't aware that he and Leonard were friends. But she was ecstatic, he remembered, not just over the commission itself, which was her biggest yet, but over the idea that an old-line firm like that could come out from behind its horsey prints and antique maps and risk hanging new work by an unknown artist in its front offices. No, he couldn't interrupt the big push she was on now to complete those pieces, and there was another discomfort besides, that held him back: he had always had the uneasy feeling that if he ever showed up at her house unexpected he might find one of her other men there. He could picture her standing on the front steps in jeans and a cotton shirt, the door pulled shut behind her, shading her eyes from the sun with one hand, telling him no, she was working, though he could see there was an unfamiliar car parked in front of her house, right in front of the fire hydrant, in fact, which he was always so careful to stay legally away from. And what could he do but smile, and apologize, and smile and back away? He could see her watching him fade predictably away into his smile. She would come down off the steps and watch him go, bit by bit, arms, legs, everything, until there was nothing left but an inane Cheshire grin, until there was nothing left behind of him but a smile that wasn't even really his, the smile of his cardboard mask.

Not knowing where else to go—his workday closed out already, his empty apartment a vortex of discomfort, anxiety, his friends all at work, children at school, everyone, everything, inaccessible—he released his grip on the door handle of his car and let himself wander back into the zoo. Only once had Elaine ever come to the zoo with him, back in the early stages of their relationship, late fall, a day just like this one for warmth and sunshine but an opposite season, the day she had first met his children, when his daughter had come up to her in the parking lot and held out her hand, acting very grown up, and said, "Hi, I'm Jennie Smith, but my name is really Cohen," and then gone prancing ahead into the zoo beside her little brother while Elaine, walking slowly beside him, kept shaking her head and saying, "Leonard, is that how you want your kids to go through life? Saying 'I am not who I really am'?" even though he had already explained the whole problem of the family name to her on their first evening together.

And in the zoo, too, he remembered how impatient she had become after the four of them had stood for some time leaning against the railing overlooking the lion exhibit, just watching the lions sleeping. On the informational panel mounted in front of the exhibit they had read, with amusement, LIONS OFTEN SLEEP AS MUCH AS TWENTY HOURS A DAY. True to form, the male and female had lain motionless on their sides, almost nose to nose, while the three cubs seemed scattered at random about the pit, as if they had just dropped to the ground wherever sleep had caught up with them. Soon, however, Elaine had turned away from the railing and gone off to sit on a bench by herself. Later, walking again, she had explained to him that it was nothing, really, that she understood the children's fascination with the lions; lovely and ferocious and asleep, they were truly beautiful animals, she had always thought so, but also she already knew them as well as she wanted to, hadn't she told him how she supported herself for several years by doing wild animal drawings for a nature magazine, of course she had.

And now the lions were sleeping again, just as, re-reading the informational panel, Leonard realized they should be: stretched out in the late-morning sun, the male and the female back to back and the three young lions, no longer cubs, in a cluster against the far rock wall, which Leonard knew from a client who had been the contractor for the zoo improvements wasn't really rock at all but a new concrete product that could be made to look like anything: brick, wood, pebbles, cliffs. But never mind, thought Leonard, the lions are asleep and comfortable, comfortable in their lion day, with its twenty hours of sleep and four to feed the flesh, comfortable in their lion careers, behind their lion masks: oh to be a lion and wear a comfortable, loose-fitting lion suit and just go on comfortably doing what one does, twenty-four hours at a time. The only thing that made him different from the lions, as far as he could tell – aside from the fact that he had the sleeping and waking ratio backwards – was that he knew he was doing it, knew every day, every hour, almost every minute, that he was zipped up in his Leonard costume, and knew moreover that it was not a good fit: that it pinched in the crotch and constricted his chest and tugged at the armpits and, of course, did terrible things around his face. Not for anything could he recall how he came to be wearing such an outfit. Even though it had the stiff feel of an off-the-rack garment from some cut-rate, direct-from-the-manufacturer outlet, Leonard knew that couldn't be the case because surely someone – a wife, a friend, a client – would have commented on such cheap goods by now. Would they have let him join the Athletic Club dressed like that? Not on your life. Nathan would have taken him aside, recommended his own tailor perhaps. But Leonard couldn't remember ever having gone for any fittings, either, couldn't remember having his measurements taken, the feel of the tape probing his crotch and circling his waist, couldn't remember looking at swatches of fabric or leafing through the pages of the style books.

So how did it come to be? he wondered: how did it come to be that I am wearing this terrible-fitting Leonard suit that owns more of my face than I do? For the first time, he truly felt the urge to talk to someone about it, though there was no one around except a young mother at the railing of the lion exhibit holding the hand of her small, look-alike daughter, who was all dressed up as if she were being taken not to the zoo but to a birthday party, wearing a red pinafore and white patent leather shoes, blond hair pulled back and tied with a shiny red ribbon.

He wanted to open his suit jacket and say to them, to someone, to anyone, "Who are these people whose name is on the label here, what is this 'Cohen & Smith, Tailors' outfit anyway? Do you know a good men's clothing shop in the vicinity? I think I must have gotten this suit for my twelfth birthday, and it no longer fits as well as it once did, as I'm sure you can see."

He didn't say anything, of course: in good part because he felt so constricted around the chest that he was afraid anything he tried to say would only come out as some raspy, unintelligible growl. But noticing that the little girl, unlike her mother, was looking not at the lions but at him, he tried, at least, a little smile. Because, however, she just kept looking at him, without the slightest change in her passive expression, he had the strange feeling, for a moment, that nothing was happening. Not even cardboard. Well, he thought, maybe I will try to say something to her after all, in a little voice, since she is a little girl. Maybe I will be able to start there.

So he knelt down, in front of her, and said, in a very soft voice, "I know why you're looking at me instead of the lions, you know."

The words came out all right, he thought, though she didn't even blink but just kept staring at him.

"It's because, " he continued, "I'm one of them, sort of."

She stared at him out of very blue eyes.

"But," he said, "I'm thinking of taking off my lion outfit any time now."

Suddenly he saw the blue eyes look up in alarm. The mother had turned away from the lions and was tugging at the child's slender arm. By the time Leonard was standing erect again, the mother was pulling the child rapidly away.

"That man says he's a lion," he could hear the little girl saying as her mother hauled her off, past the tiger and leopard exhibits, in the direction of the monkey house, "and do you know what he says he's going to do?"

"You just be a pussycat," he could hear the mother say, "and follow me."

What Would I Know?

FOR MY OWN sake, I would like you to think that it all started out in innocence and exuberance – the Fourth of July seems like an ideal time for that. But I cannot seem to make it come out quite that way. Not that there wasn't some of both around at the beginning, though perhaps there shouldn't have been. They had both been through painful marriages and difficult divorces and the messy stuff that comes during and after. You would have thought they would have known better, and in fact I am sure they did, both of them. Maybe they just decided to put away what they knew for awhile, and then forgot to go and collect it again. Or maybe they didn't decide, maybe they just did. Or maybe they didn't even know what they knew, if you get what I mean. Or to put it another way, maybe they didn't really know what they thought they knew. I don't know, these things are hard to figure out.

So however things worked out later, I would say that they came to my Fourth of July party not with any naiveté but even, I suppose, with a certain malice aforethought – though probably what each of them had thought about beforehand was nothing more malicious than trying to figure out how to get laid that evening. Not by each other, of course; they didn't know each other yet.

I could see what was going on with him as soon as the guests began to arrive. He had been staying with me for a couple of days, had spent most of the time in a lawn chair, relaxing and reading and drinking and talking to me, and had been of absolutely no help with the party preparations. But the arrival of the first guests seemed to spur him to a flurry of activity, as if he had suddenly remembered what he was here for after all. One moment he was at the front window, looking to see who was pulling up, and the next he was lumbering toward the back, to see if anyone had slipped through without his knowing it. People had to pass through the house to get to the back yard, where I had laid out a sizable spread of food and drink less as a celebration of the national holiday than as a welcome-home party for the old friend that he was, and he could have simply sat out there basking in the hot, late-afternoon sun and his role as honored guest. Instead, he lingered in the shadowy house, singling out, one by one, the women as they came through. He wasn't aggressive, but he was large and unkempt, and size and shagginess can create a certain sense of intimidation which I would like to say he used without even being aware that he used it. That would make it seem more innocent. And perhaps it was even the truth, that lack of awareness of what he was doing, but I am no longer as willing as I once was to equate ignorance with innocence.

I myself was drifting through the middle of an affair with a tall and elegantly beautiful woman whom I couldn't seem to manage to fall in love with. At the time, of course, I didn't know it was the middle of our affair, I thought it was still somewhere near the beginning, and that there was plenty of time left and therefore hope. Actually, it was probably already nearer the end than the middle. However, as is usually the case, I suspect, neither of us was at that time particularly aware of the stage of our relationship, and so we bustled rather happily around each other in my kitchen and on the back porch, filling people's hands with drinks and making the necessary introductions. She had brought her best friend along.

This was a woman I had met on several previous occasions, and, though I wasn't particularly taken with her personally, I was happy enough to add her to the party, not just as Kate's friend, though that would have been reason enough, but for her own liveliness of spirit and conversational intensity. *She* was aggressive. She didn't need introductions, though she was the only real stranger at the party, since I had primarily invited old friends of his and mine to visit with him after his absence of several years. But she was quick to leap up from the picnic bench or one of the blankets I had spread on the back lawn, to greet newcomers and introduce herself with a handshake that, if she hadn't exercised considerable restraint, could have brought some of my strongest guests down on their knees in the freshly cut grass. I had seen her use it before to make sure things got started out on her own terms, and it convinced me she knew what she was doing.

The two of them didn't exactly fall into each other's arms the moment they were introduced. They met in the kitchen, where she had come in, maybe feeling for a moment – though she would have gotten a quick enough grip on herself to make sure the feeling didn't last long – just a bit at a loss among all these strangers, to ask if she could be of any help. I was handing her the large relish tray I had prepared when he came through from the back yard in hot pursuit of my ex-wife, who had made her brief-as-usual appearance and was on her way out, winking at me on her passage through the kitchen.

"Jim," I said, reaching out to stop him with a tug at the elbow, "this is Molly."

"Oh hi," he said, but I don't think he even looked at her, though her red hair was hard to ignore. He was focused elsewhere, and she, for her part, was so laden down with that enormous tray full of olives and celery and carrots and green onions and cucumbers and broccoli flowers that she didn't have a free hand to extend to him, which was probably just as well. I held open the screen door so she could carry the tray out to the picnic table, and by the time I got back into the kitchen to finish collecting the sausages I was going to grill, I could see through the window that out in the street in front of the house Jim had my ex-wife in a bear hug that could easily have passed for old-friendship-affectionateness. But I could also see from the way she squirmed out of his huge grasp and dove into the safety of her little VW that it wasn't. She was always quick. She was also very big on self-awareness, at least as a concept.

At the time I felt that most of the people I knew fell into one or the other of only two categories: those who had no notion of what self-awareness was, and no self-awareness, either; and those who were very keen on the idea of self-awareness but wholly deluded about themselves. I hadn't the foggiest notion as to which category I fit into myself. I wasn't even sure I was interested in knowing. As far as I could see, the great contemporary quest for self-awareness wasn't doing any of my friends a whole lot of good. But ignorance, as I had discovered in my own marriage, didn't seem to help a great deal either. Given a choice, I would have stayed away from the whole messy subject and just gone on about the business of daily living, but some things, I guess, there is just no avoiding, especially with people like Jim and Molly around. They were just about to get acquainted, and I was just about to begin to have to wonder what this process of getting acquainted – with others, with oneself – was really all about.

Meanwhile, Kate, who never missed a thing, was not pleased to see me keeping such a watchful eye on my ex-wife and so had yanked another beer out of the refrigerator, making just enough commotion about it to make sure I wouldn't miss it, and charged out into the backyard, where the rest of the crowd was gathered. I was never much motivated to follow trouble too closely behind, so I hung around the kitchen awhile, gathering up the sausages and the rest of the makings for dinner. Finally Jim shambled back in, half his shirt tucked in and half hanging out over his sizable belly, and I got him to help me carry the food out. Kate and Molly were standing, talking, next to the grill, where the coals were already glowing. This time, while we were setting the food down, Jim saw her.

She was the kind of woman other women always tell you is attractive, the kind they always say could be really beautiful if only she'd lose some weight. I don't think so myself, but what would I know? I have always been attracted to tall, slender women with legs like sticks and hardly any breasts. And proper, painless handshakes. Anyway, I imagine we will never have an opportunity to test the theory of Molly's beauty potential because she was a solid chunk of humanity even then and has continued to expand ever since their marriage, along with Jim, whose own capacity for expansion seems unlimited. Every time we have lunch together, Jim and I, he tells me that they are both dieting, though from the size of his lunch and his stomach I am inclined to be a little dubious about that. But what would I know? I am the kind of fellow they used to refer to as puny, and lunch for me is less a time to eat than a chance to escape the office and chat with old friends.

At our lunches he also tells me how happy he is. He tells me that a lot. And he tells me with regularity what a wonderful handshake she has.

That first night that they met in my kitchen and back yard they ended up spending in my bed, though I don't want to make too much of my generosity since Kate was perfectly willing to have me come to her apartment so that she could continue to show me in a variety of ways that I could fall in love with her easily enough if I would only let myself. That was her point of view, not mine. I think we might all have been better off if we had slept in our own beds that night, but who am I to say? Kate's opinion of me to the contrary, it was a time in my life when I was perfectly willing to let almost anything happen. I did ask Molly and Jim, when the rest of the guests had left and Kate and I were about to take off for her apartment, to please remember to let the dog out before they went to sleep, but along with the whiskey spills and dirty glasses and overflowing ashtrays and the unmade bed, there was smelly evidence in the morning when I returned that they had not been paying a lot of attention to my request. I have never been very big on cleaning up other peoples' messes.

They were both gone by the time I got back that morning – she had her job to get to and he had planned to get an early start on the next leg of the summer trip he was making – and I didn't see either of them again until their wedding a few months later. It all sounds very romantic, I suppose, especially when you remember that they were both middle-aged people, with long dreary marriages behind them and grown children still around them, and here on the Fourth of July, in my own small, fenced-in back yard, in the midst of picnic blankets and beer drinkers and sizzling bratwurst, they had discovered each other. And a future. It turned out they had managed quite a lot of contact in the intervening months. She had wrangled some excuse of a business trip to go east to see him. He had returned to spend three whole weeks holed up in her house later in the summer, along with her mother and daughter and numerous cats and dogs, without letting another soul know he was back in town. They had met somewhere in between for a long weekend early in the fall, and even in their separate cities they had met nightly, for long hours, on the telephone. It seemed awfully quick to me all the same, but what would I know? Because it is in such contrast to the way I generally find myself just drifting in and out of things, I have always believed that when other people take this sort of decisive action, they must surely know what they're doing. And if they don't, I'm not sure I want to know that, though sometimes such knowledge seems to be thrust upon us whether we want it or not.

The wedding party consisted of their children and her mother, Kate and myself, and a few other old friends on both sides. It took place at Molly's house, so the animals were present, too, and somewhere or other, neither of them being especially religious, they had rounded up an aging hippie sort of Unitarian minister, the kind you used to find tagging along after the flower children and street people on the fringes of university districts back in the sixties. They had gotten him to leave his beads home for the occasion. He was no problem because they had written their own ceremony, naturally. Poetry and pledges. A friend played the flute. Even while they were standing in front of the fireplace with the minister between them, Jim's shirt seemed to creep up out of his pants on its own. We were too small a group for a reception line, but Molly went around and shook everyone's hand when the ceremony was over, with a grip that demonstrated just how certain she was about this. Jim went around giving everyone his great bear hug. Even Kate, who was on the whole quite a tough cookie and as cynical about everyone else's relationship as she was about the one we were clearly struggling with by then, was touched.

"Maybe they're the smart ones," she said, "for taking the risk and letting something happen."

She said that to me quite a few times, both during the ceremony and afterwards, though not nearly so many times, I suspect, as she would have liked. Looking back, I have to admire her for not saying it more often and for not jabbing me in the ribs every time she said it. Self-restraint was not generally one of her strong points, though you would never have known it to see her trim, straight figure and elegant silver-grey suit and every hair in place.

Anyway, every time she said that I nodded. The dogs ran around the living room and barked and knocked over the music stand, the minister stood in front of the fireplace with a Bible open in his hands as if the ceremony were still going on, the daughter announced that she was going down to her room in the basement to smoke a joint and that anyone who wanted could join her, and Kate told me about the smart ones and I nodded. It was certainly not a nod of agreement, and I do not even think it was a cynical oh-sure-can't-you-see-I-know-better-than-that nod of self-awareness. I neither knew better than that nor didn't know better than that. I think probably it was just one of those nods that said, Yeah, I hear you,

you don't have to say it again. Off and on, though, even after the wedding, through the last couple of months of our affair, she said it again. Maybe she was right. I wouldn't know. If it's Jim and Molly we're talking about, I am on the outside looking in, though obviously I have some doubts or I wouldn't be trying to piece it all together like this. If it is myself we are talking about, which is not really the purpose of this, all I can say is that I am on the inside looking out and I do not find the view a whole lot clearer. But I am not even sure if that is something I should be interested in. After all, I was just a bystander in these events. And if it is Kate we are talking about, I am sorry to say that I have not seen her at all in some time now. I would like to think that maybe by now she has found that she was right for herself, anyway. But I think that maybe she is too cautious for that – that she, too, is something of a bystander, though to be sure a far more energetic one than myself. There are passive bystanders and active bystanders, and she was one of the latter, grabbing at this or that as it passed by but as ignorant as myself, I suspect, when it came to knowing what for or deciding to abandon the reviewing stand and join the parade marching down the street in front of her.

Jim and Molly, of course, would have agreed with her right away, if she had delivered her regulation one-liner to them, which I am sure she did after she and I split up and she began to see a lot more of them on her own than she and I ever did together, though I don't really think I can be faulted for that, since she and I weren't together for very long after Jim and Molly got married.

Well, I don't mean to be going on so about Kate and myself when it's really Jim and Molly I've been trying to figure out. This is their story, not ours, not mine. We weren't either of us, Kate or I, the kind to be walking wide-eyed and exuberant into anything, that is pure deadly and we both knew it, you've got to have blinders on and a sheet draped over your mirror as well to do it that way, which is what I hear some people actually do with mirrors when there's been a death in the house. I think Jim and Molly probably just don't have any mirrors in their house. You look the way I see Jim looking these days, and you wouldn't want a *lot* of mirrors around, anyway.

"We've given up drinking, too," he told me at lunch a few months ago.

Just then the waitress came by and asked, "You want another glass of wine, Mr. P.?"

I was late and busy hanging up my coat and hat and getting settled in the booth, so I didn't say anything. What would I know, anyway? I can't handle anything stronger than coffee when I'm working.

So he sipped on his port wine, which would not be my idea of what to drink with lunch if I drank at lunchtime, and I filled my coffee cup the rest of the way up with cream and sugar, and when we were done ordering—I just had soup, but he had the luncheon special, mashed potatoes and gravy and all—he started in telling me all about the work he was doing enlarging their bedroom. Knocking out walls, adding fifteen feet to one end, practically moving out into the back yard, new windows, insulation, roofing. I've always admired people who could tackle projects like that. I wouldn't even know how to begin, myself. Putting up a new light fixture pretty much stretches the limits of my mechanical abilities. And doing a job like that on the bedroom sounded somehow really important to me. I knew he had redone the bathroom last year, but that wasn't the same, the bathroom was a room everybody in the house used, even the cats in that house. The bedroom was a job he was doing just for himself and Molly.

When he was done with his carpentry monologue, which filled up most of the lunch hour, I told him that he sounded real good, that he sounded happy with his new life.

He wiped the gravy spills off his shirt front and said, "Sure. Why shouldn't I be?"

If you think I'm going to end up telling you that the new ceiling joists collapsed on him, thereby bringing him his just desserts for staking so much of his life on the reconstruction of the bridal chamber, or that the foundations of the marriage itself suddenly began to crumble, or that one or the other of them has been going around sounding perfectly miserable but determined to hang on no matter what winds are whistling in around the poorly framed windows, or even that one of the cats died, you are wrong. If any one of those things was the case, I would have given it to you straight out at the beginning and then tried to go back and figure it out from there. I am no withholder of crucial information and I do not believe in surprises, which, as I have observed all too often, only tend to bring shock and dismay and sometimes anger even when they were intended to delight. I don't even like suspense, it's just that sometimes you can't quite get to the end of things. It is true that one of the dogs ran away a few days ago and hasn't been seen since, but it may well be back by now and I don't think that is exactly the sort of stuff we're interested in here, anyway. No doubt the new, expanded bedroom isn't finished yet either—from all I have ever heard, projects like that always take at least twice as long as you've figured they will—but what of it?

No, what I'm really thinking is that nothing has changed. Oh, he used to call her "my bride" for the first year or so of their marriage, and now he refers to her by her first name. I would consider that an improvement. And the house is changing, of course. And the daughter's boyfriend has moved in and the two of them have set up a sort of housekeeping arrangement in the basement, emerging from time to time to use the kitchen and the new bathroom and, of course, paying no rent. One of the cats has had two litters of kittens. So things are pretty much the same, except more so. There is more of everything, even of Jim and Molly. I'm not knocking it— some people do better with more, I suppose, and some with less— only I am wondering if more is what either of them thought they were signing up for on that innocent-seeming evening in my back yard, and in the months that followed when, as Kate kept putting it, they got smart and let themselves take the risk.

I wouldn't know, I suppose, since I am not one of the ones who got smart and took the risk. I was the one who just stood by watching things happen and trying to stay out of trouble, which is far less charming and romantic and risky, as Kate spent most of our last night together telling me, in between times of showing me that I could still have my chances. I give her credit for a lot of perseverance, and also for knowing when the end was the end. If I ever see her again, I would like to tell her how sorry I am that she drifted into this relationship with the kind of person who wasn't able to take the risks that she wanted me to take with her. To do that I would have had to know myself either a lot more or a lot less: enough either to know what I wanted to leave the sidelines for, what kind of participant I could choose to be, or not enough to know that I should just stay on the sidelines. As it was, I was in the middle somewhere. I wouldn't say I was a total idiot about myself, but I guess I couldn't say I had a lot of perspective on the issue, either. I wouldn't know, really.

I do think, though, that if I was, as Kate says, going to be smart and take the risks, that smart for me would not consist of taking risks for more of the same. I do know myself some, you see, and though I do not have anything against what I know of me, I don't see what's in it for me to go all out just for more of the same. I do not want to simply hang on to what I already have with a firm handshake and keep squeezing until I bring my life to its knees. I do not want to see my belly slowly pushing my shirt out over my belt buckle as the years go by. If that's what I want, why take risks? For the same, I can be comfortable right where I am. In fact, all I have to do is stay put, and that's exactly what I'll get, though maybe not quite as much more as Jim and Molly have gotten. No, if I am going to take risks, it would have to be, as I tried to tell Kate the last time we were together, back at the beginning of the year, not for more but for different, though that turned out to be much harder for me to explain than I expected. Maybe I just haven't got it down right yet. I don't know.

This last time I am talking about was the *last* last time we were together, not the last night I was talking about before, which was the last night in a different way. This time we were in New York, separately but at the same conference, and had run into each other in the lobby of the hotel where the meetings were being held and had had our drink together at the hotel bar in the name of old friendship and as had happened almost every time over the past year since our affair had ended and when we got together to talk about how we could still be good friends, we had ended up in bed. In her room. And then we had talked about Jim and Molly. About everybody's houses and children, including hers and mine. About fat and thin. About cautions and risks.

And then I said, "I would not want to be them."

She squinted at me the way she always did when she had her contacts out, as if she had to really concentrate to make sure she was seeing what she was seeing, and said, "So who asked you to?"

I told her my theory about more or different.

"So I was more and you wanted different?" she said. She pulled the covers up to her chin. "What did you want? Some sixteen-year-old black girl? Some little cheerleader with big tits? A whole fucking harem?"

"I think you're missing the point," I told her.

"I know I'm missing the point," she said. "Do you know what you're missing?"

Well, I thought, if I was missing what Jim and Molly had found, then I was just as happy to be missing it. If I was missing something else, I wouldn't know, would I, since it was missing. I did think I knew myself well enough by then to know that I would know what I was missing if it ever came around, but I did not think that Kate was what I was missing. She was too much like me, which was cer-

tainly something I did not mind – we could be good friends, me and
the just-like-me – but certainly did not want a whole lot more of,
either. There are a lot more things I might have thought, too – I was
sitting up in the middle of her bed by then, thinking that I was right
on the verge of really figuring this thing out at last. I thought maybe
I was finally about to get to the end of this question about just how
much you have to know about yourself to know what you really
wanted and how to go after it, to know it was time to step off the
curb and cross the street to get to what you really wanted, not to
know so much that you just grabbed onto the nearest pedestrian
with the certainty that you knew it all already so why cross over,
but not to be so dumb, either, that you got run over in traffic without knowing what hit you, I almost had it there for a moment, I
think, though what would I know, really – only just then Kate
reached out from under the covers and kicked them off and pulled
me down on top of her.

"Do it to me again," she said, "I don't care if it is only more of
the same."

Sue: A Meditation on History

THE ABANDONED CABIN was a full hour's hike in from the highway, up a steep and barely visible path that I never would have found without the clues my friends, the Gordons, who lived in the area, had given me. The trail was rocky in some places and swamp-soggy in others and, everywhere, on the rise. Then, just as it seemed ready at last to peter out completely, it trickled over the edge of the ridge and down toward the lake and the abandoned cabin. I wasn't interested in the cabin, or what was left of it. This is hard country up here, dotted all over with the abandoned hopes of people who had come long ago for the dream of a seasonal retreat or perhaps even with visions of making a year-round go of it. But the weather here is never easy, access is difficult, supplies hard to come by. The snow arrives early and stays late, and you find, soon enough, that your mind is always focused on the question of survival. I don't think that's anyone's true dream.

But the lake was everything the Gordons had promised. Not big, maybe a quarter of a mile long, a hundred yards across where I stood, but opening out to several times that down at the far end, where I could see how it curved around a rocky outcropping. I had climbed through a birch forest most of the way up the trail, but here it was cedar and spruce and red pine that surrounded the lake and sometimes hung out over it. Across the lake from where I stood was

93

the rocky cliff, maybe two hundred feet high, where the eagles nested. I didn't see the eagles but I didn't need to, either. It was enough to know that they nested there. At the foot of the cliff was a rockslide area, great granite chunks that had broken off and tumbled to the very edge of the lake, some of them no doubt hidden in the water. In front of the rockslide a loon was swimming. I watched it till it dove, tried to guess where it would finally come up, was wrong, tried again, was wrong again. When it laughed I was so sure it was laughing at me that I sat down on a fallen log and laughed with it. I looked at the base of the log and saw that it hadn't fallen by accident, but had been felled by beavers, chewed to a point, just like the stump nearby. But it had wedged, when it fell, between a couple of other trees and they had apparently not been able to remove it. Down at the far end of the lake, where it looked swampy, where perhaps the inlet or the outlet flowed, I thought I could make out the low hump of the beavers' house, but I couldn't be certain at that distance. It didn't make a lot of difference, it was out there somewhere. I supposed I should have brought my fishing tackle, as the Gordons had suggested, but I'm not sure I would have used it.

Eventually I got up off the beaver-felled log and wandered over to the abandoned cabin, which wasn't much: its windows out, its plank siding weathered grey and frail-looking, the whole side nearest me punched full of holes from having been used for target practice, probably by some frustrated hunter who'd been told he couldn't hit the broad side of a barn. He'd hit the narrow side of the cabin with considerable accuracy. The steps were gone and so was the door and so, as I could see when I stuck my head in, was part of the floor, where, from the look of the charred floorboards, someone had been building fires right in the middle of the cabin's one room. On the back wall, just beyond the burn-hole, deeply carved in letters nearly a foot tall, it said

SUE

X

KEN

And lower down toward the other side of the same wall, where lots of light came in because it was the wall that had been so effectively punctured by shotgun blasts, a smaller set of carvings read

SUE

X

FRANK

And over in the far corner, on the wall just beyond the hole in the ceiling where once the stovepipe must have gone, though there was no longer any sign of the stove, it said, in letters almost as large as the first ones I'd seen,

SUE

X

BOBBY

I pulled my head and shoulders back out of the cabin doorway, feeling I could be pretty certain that this cabin had never belonged to Sue or any of her friends, though they had obviously been willing to go to a lot of trouble to get to it. Stepping back, I could see, recognizing it from its rusted hinges, where the door had been shoved half out of sight under the front edge of the cabin, which was propped up on rocks maybe a foot or so off the ground. In upsidedown lettering carved so deeply it looked like it should have gone nearly through the wooden slats of the door, Sue announced her name once more, but whoever was with her this time was lost in the dark shadows beneath the abandoned cabin.

2.

After I bought the place, I debated with myself for a long time about whether to fix up the existing cabin or tear it down and start building from scratch. I suppose there was yet a third choice, namely to leave the abandoned cabin as it was and build somewhere else on the forty acres or so I'd purchased that bordered the western and southern shores of the lake. But whoever had built this cabin had selected, as I'm sure he must have known and as any fool could have seen on even the briefest inspection of the area, the one obviously perfect building site. On a gentle slope set thirty feet or so back from the water's edge, it commanded a sweeping view of the entire lake, excepting only the outer reaches of the far, wider end. The tall cliff across the lake protected it from the western winds, the rocky hill to the right from the bitter northern winds, and the slight ridge behind from the damp and freezing winds that sometimes swept up into the hills off nearby Lake Superior. If it was open to the frequent northwest winds sweeping in at it across the lake, between the cliff and the rocky hillside, why, that was only a reminder of reality, of the harsh weather, the long winters, of this northern world.

And where else could a cabin have gone? Up against that rocky hillside, perhaps, for yet greater protection against the weather, but only at the expense of losing a considerable portion of the lake view. Surely not back on the other side of the ridge, where, though the birch forest was lovely, there was no view at all to be had of the lake. Right up on the crest of the ridge was a possibility, but its dual blessing of viewing the birches in one direction and the lake in the other could be purchased only at the cost of exposing the cabin to winter winds from every direction, a choice no prospective resident in his right mind could possibly have made. And down toward the south end of the lake the land settled into a gentle depression, shady, mossy, quiet, and unbuildable: a bog.

So the only question that remained was not *where*, but *what*.

Either way, I knew, would involve considerable effort simply in getting the building materials up to the site, though even while I was busy mulling over my choices I occupied myself for several weeks by working on the lower elevations of the trail, widening and firming it, cutting trees and packing dirt in the wet spots, so that a sturdy four-wheel-drive vehicle could get at least halfway in to the lake. Beyond that, given the steep grade of the hill, the rocky terrain, and the streams that angled this way and that across the slope, it would have taken earth-moving equipment to do the job, and I had no desire to see bulldozers and backhoes despoiling my wilderness.

When I wasn't working on improving my access road, I spent a lot of time both sitting on the log the beavers had so conveniently provided for me and wandering in and out of and around the abandoned cabin. It wasn't really in such decrepit condition as it looked on first glance. I examined the stone footings and found them solid, pounded at the plank siding and found the boards sound, except where they'd been burned away by indoor fires or punched with holes by shotgun blasts. And that sort of damage could easily be repaired; I would have redone the flooring in any case, and insulated and closed in the sidewalls, too, which were only a shell as it stood, with exposed studs. And the studs were solid, the beams that supported the building twice the thickness they needed to be. Not a sign of rot in the joists. The roof, of course, needed to be replaced, but that was no problem; the beams were all sound. Whoever had built this cabin had known what he was doing, at least when it came to building a cabin.

A new cabin, of course, would give me a certain freedom of choice, the right to design a cabin according to my own ideas, and as I sat on the log looking sometimes out toward the lake and other times back toward the building site, with a sketching pad balanced on my knees, I drafted a good many possibilities. They tended on the whole toward more contemporary designs, some interestingly

97

different materials, expansion of the living space. If tearing down the old cabin before starting on the new presented something of a preliminary hurdle, I could see, at least, that many of the sound timbers from the old could be reused in the new, so that on the whole building anew would not be vastly more expensive than reclaiming the old, nor would getting materials to the site involve much more labor. Tearing down the old cabin would take some work, but that would be offset to a great extent by my being able to reuse the lumber that was already here instead of hauling in new beams and joists and studs. It was, as the Gordons told me in the time-honored cliché as I sat at their kitchen table with them, drinking thin coffee and explaining my dilemma, six of one and half-a-dozen of the other.

Sue made the decision for me.

3.

I was in the nearest town, about a dozen miles away, sitting in Karen's Kafe drinking coffee – koffee, I kept thinking – and trying to dry out. It had been raining all week, raining at night on the few occasions when it had cleared up during the day but mostly just keeping at it day and night, with a steady drizzle that would unpredictably turn into a heavy downpour, often just when there looked to be a break in the overcast. I had worked in the rain, clearing the trail, cutting firewood, hauling debris out from under the cabin. I had cooked in the rain and tramped around my small domain in the rain and sat on my beaver log watching the lake in the rain, hoping for an eagle to appear, wondering what had become of the loon. And I had slept in the rain, too, almost literally the preceding night, when the small tent I had pitched beside the abandoned cabin had at last absorbed all the moisture its canvas could hold and begun to precipitate a fine spray inside. Everything I had with me was wet; the clothes I was wearing were wet, my socks and underwear were wet, somehow even the inside of my car, which I had parked off the highway at the foot of my trail, was wet, even though the windows had been tightly rolled up. And it was still raining, as I could see out the window while Karen herself—her name stitched in blue script across the cream-colored blouse she wore—refilled my coffee cup. Koffee kup, I reminded myself, trying to prove, if only to myself, that I still hadn't lost my sense of humor.

Karen, middle-aged, chubby, solicitous—the perfect sort of person to be running a small-town coffee shop where everyone seemed to know everyone else—seemed happy, though, as well she should have been, since her place was packed at mid-morning. The week of continuous rain seemed to have driven everyone indoors, unless, I realized, they'd been happily warming their stomachs with Karen's hot coffee all week while only I, like a fool, had stuck to my labors in the rain. But this was a world of men who worked outdoors—for the logging companies, in the lumber mills, on the railroad, with the forest service—and who turned to the outdoors even when they weren't working—hunting and fishing and snowmobiling. They were husky, healthy-looking men, even the grey-haired ones among them, and big men, too, all of them bigger than me, and looking even bigger than they were in the heavy clothes they wore: wide rubber boots, open at the top; quilted jackets, also open, showing the plaid woolen shirts beneath; hats kept on even indoors; heavy canvas or suede work gloves stuffed in back pockets. They filled Karen's place, which was a good-sized restaurant for a small town like this, completely. I was at the counter, near the cash register, but these men had every table occupied, and Karen's little crew of waitresses, highschool girls, most of them, probably serving their fathers and brothers and uncles, scooted about between the tables with coffeepots in both hands, pouring everwhere they saw a half-drained cup, not even waiting to be asked.

They were dressed just like Karen: blue skirts, cream-colored blouses, their names stitched in blue script just above the left breast. And as they passed back and forth near me, slipping behind

99

the counter where I sat to refill their serving pots from the big urns back there, I began after an hour or so, almost inadvertently, to know them by name. The tall, thin girl with the golden hair was Elke, and the one who might have passed for her sister, though she was a full foot shorter, was another Karin, with an *i*. The only adult woman beside Karen herself was Emilia. The other girls were Inga and Kari and Kristine. The cook, who appeared from time to time to set out an order in the opening between the kitchen and the counter, didn't wear a blouse with her name on it, but I heard the waitresses address her as Clara. Or maybe it was Klara. This was basically Scandinavian-settled country I was in, as I had known all along without thinking much about it. Finns and Germans at the very least. The men, I was sure—I had overheard them call each other here, listened to the Gordons talking about their friends and neighbors, met them with names on their uniforms in gas stations— were Lars and Sven and Kurt and Eino. The women were Solveig and Gretchen and Helvig and Ilsa. Thrtr were no Pats, no Marys, no Melissas or Cindys here. No Sues.

4.

I suppose I could have cut out the planks on which Sue's name had been carved with her friends, her Bobbys and Kennys and Franks. I never did learn whose name had been intended to meet up with hers on the back of the door. When I pulled the door out from beneath the cabin, I found that all that had been carved in it was

SUE

X

and nothing more. It seemed, when I looked at it, that that probably hadn't been such a good time—interrupted, frustrated, uncompleted. Someone who had long dreamed of going up to the abandoned cabin with Sue—some Billy or Joe or Paul—had perhaps ended his brief escapade by kicking out the door in rage, taking his satisfaction from seeing it fly off its rusted hinges, leaving Sue to toss it underneath on some subsequent visit. Maybe, though, it had just been some unexpected intrusion, a group of hunters stumbling onto the scene, that had caused Billy or Joe or Paul to abandon the carving that had already gouged Sue's name so deeply into the wood. And perhaps, it occurred to me, it was Sue herself, Sue alone, the door already fallen from the frame of its own accord and Sue sitting beside it on the pine-needle-strewn ground outside the cabin, knife in hand, making her mark, preparing to record the future, leaving the final item on her document blank and sliding it, for protection, just under the front edge of the cabin, beside the empty doorframe, within easy reach. I wondered if she'd ever come back to the cabin again after that time, ever made that strenuous climb – perhaps not so strenuous, after all, they were young and well-motivated – with Kenny again or with someone new, some Mike or Mark. But ultimately it didn't make any difference to me whether Kenny's name had been recorded there on his first visit with Sue or only after they had spent a couple of years making the climb up there together. It didn't make any difference whether the three names and one blank I found recorded there represented the only three or four times Sue herself had visited the abandoned cabin or whether they were the merest surface manifestations of a long and active and for the most part undocumented career. Whatever it was that Sue had constructed here . . . "constructed" doesn't seem like exactly the right word, perhaps "created" or "invented" would be better, but I like "constructed" all the same because it seems to connect her with the original building of the cabin, long before her time no doubt. Anyway, whatever it was she had constructed here – fantasy, romance, simple lust, hard work, maybe even marriage finally – whatever it was, in this alien environment of beavers and loons and eagles, hard climbs and icy winds, Scandinavians and shotgun-blasted walls, whatever it was, I knew *I* wasn't about to pull it down. Or even alter it drastically.

Briefly, when the rain stopped and I came back from my over-night stay in a motel, resuscitated by a dry bed and a hot shower, to take up residence in my tent once again, I did give some thought to the possibility of sawing out the planks that bore Sue's record, then saving them to hang, perhaps even framed, either in the new cabin I built or the old one I rebuilt. But it occurred to me almost at once what a preposterous notion that was. I only wanted to preserve the world that Sue had constructed, not to display it, not to make a curiosity, or, worse yet, a guessing game, a travesty, of it. And to whom would I display it, anyway? The absent eagle and unseen beavers? The long-departed loon? For myself, I would always know what was there now, even though I blanketed the deep inscriptions under insulation and then covered the insulation with interior paneling. Even though I hung pictures of my own on the walls, which I somehow could not imagine doing, or notched them with the record of my own days. No more than Sue had torn down the previous builder's cabin to make way for her own new world could I dis-assemble Sue's world in order to clear the way for mine. No, like Sue I could begin with what was there, I could build on what was there however little I truly understood of it and however much my layering-on might gradually obliterate its traces. I could live with what I would always know was there.

I kind of liked that idea. Besides, the cedar planks of the walls and door, cedar planks from trees doubtless felled and hewn close by this very site, were solid. Solid, aged, well-dried planks, better than you could find in a lumberyard today. Even the door, which had lain beneath the cabin propped up, by accident in all likelihood, on small rocks, and so protected from the rotting damp of the ground.

5.

Ultimately, I suspected, that was all any of us wanted: protection, for a while, from the rotting damp of the ground. The eagles I still hadn't seen, making their nest high up on – in – the rocky face of the cliff, and the beavers, too, who had left the lakeshore littered with gnawed evidence of their slightly perverse habits of making their snug homes right in the water. The loon I didn't know about. But Sue of course. And myself as well. As soon as I'd made up my mind what I was going to do, I dismantled my tent, spread it like a tarp over the roof of the abandoned cabin to secure me from leaks in the next rainstorm, and laid out my sleeping bag and various bundles of belongings on the cabin floor, which was quite solid everywhere except where the fires had been built directly on it and had left a charred hole several feet in diameter. When the weather was good I made my morning coffee and cooked my evening meal outside, and sat on my beaver log looking at the lake while I ate. When, as was more often the case, the weather was less amiable – when it was raining or threatening to, when the cold wind came across the lake out of the northwest, or when, as happened occasionally, it snowed lightly – I set my little camp stove up inside, pretty much where I figured the kitchen used to be.

Work kept me warm during the day, and my good down sleeping bag did the job at night. Evenings, I tended to bundle up as needed in most of what I'd brought with me, layering myself in shirts and sweaters, though there were also evenings when it was possible to sit down by the lake in nothing more than jeans and a t-shirt, slapping mosquitoes and watching the sun sink behind the cliff across the way. I wasn't exactly ready for winter, but I had several months to prepare myself and my cabin for that. And in the meantime I had been given every reasonable assurance by the Gordons and the other local residents I had begun to meet as I got involved with purchasing supplies for living and working here – at the grocery (Johannsen's), at the hardware store (Sven's A–1), at Nels Soderberg's small lumber mill and at Urho's Standard Station – that the coming month, July, was the one month of the year when I could rest assured that it never snowed. As far as anyone could remember.

6.

The Gordons, Sonny and Kiki. She was small, dark-haired, quick-witted and quick-tongued, a maker of thin coffee. He was not much taller, thinning brown hair, witty also but in more of a slow, wry fashion, brewer of a richer pot. They'd have been just as happy to serve me Coke or beer or brandy, and did at times, but usually it was coffee we drank together, Kiki jumping up to put the pot on as soon as I came in, exclaiming all the while that she was no good at it, that she never seemed to be able to get it right. But off she went to do it all the same, never suggesting that her husband might make it, and Sonny all the while sitting wherever he'd been sitting when I came in, and never offering to make it, never suggesting what she might try to get it right, never just getting up and putting the pot on himself, except on the few occasions when he was the only one home when I arrived.

I suppose, as an acquaintance back in the city once remarked when I was telling her about my friends who lived up on the North Shore of Lake Superior, that there was something slightly odd about their names. That traditional English, or was it Scottish, surname, with a couple of rather silly, Hollywood-of-the-thirties nicknames appended to it. She admitted, on second thought, that they were perhaps not unlike the names one found in novels by Evelyn Waugh, or other works dealing with the English aristocracy in the years just before and after the First World War. But I knew that wasn't it either. I knew – not because I'd ever inquired, but because I remembered Sonny having brought it up once himself, many years ago, in the early days of our friendship, when we'd been discussing family backgrounds – that the name hadn't really been Gordon anyway. It had been something complexly Polish or Russian or Germanic, the sort of name our nineteenth-century immigration officers had little patience for and less ability to spell. And so Gorymski or Grotowskowitz or Guertenbrecker had become, with an easy slash of a pen, Gordon. Like many another third- or fourth-generation American, Sonny had at one time expressed a mild desire to have his real name back, but there was a lot of work involved in that, a lot of research to begin with, and in the end probably a lot of confusion, too, what with going through all the complications of a name change: credit cards and bank accounts, telephone listings, social security, friends, children and their friends. Not easy. I supposed that Sonny had never taken any actual steps in that direction, beyond raising the usual questions in the family. I don't know. He never mentioned it again.

Nor did he ever mention anything about either his or Kiki's nicknames. In fact, for all I knew, they weren't nicknames. It just wasn't the sort of thing I would ever have thought of inquiring about. Whatever anyone told me his or her name was, was always good enough for me. I never felt under any compulsion to say "My, how odd," or to ask if it was an old family name, a mother's maiden name, a holdover from childhood, something foreign, whatever. A name was just what someone was to be called by, as far as I was concerned, not a sort of scruff of the neck to take people and shake them by.

No more did it occur to me to ask further about Sue's name. Susan, Suzanne, or Suzanna, what difference did it make? I even knew a Sunita once, whose parents had been India scholars; she was Sunita at home but Sue everywhere else. Sue was Sue, as the multitude of carvings on the walls and door of my cabin testified, and that was all there was to it. I had no doubt that she had a last name as well as a first, but since she hadn't chosen to sign in with it, I couldn't find that it was of any interest to me. I was somehow glad—is "glad" the right word?—well, glad then, to have what there was of her there, just as I was glad to have Sonny and Kiki, and didn't need any more of them than what they gave me.

The only curious thing was Sonny's remarking as the three of us sat around drinking coffee one evening when I'd journeyed down from my hills and my labor to their lakeshore house, that he'd never noticed any names carved on the walls of that old, abandoned cabin. He'd been the one, after all, who'd suggested my hiking up there in the first place. He'd been the one who'd told me how much luck he used to have fishing for walleye up there and how beautiful Kiki had found the spot the first time he'd taken her along with him, how she'd just stood there admiring it and had never even thrown her line in all morning. He sat across the kitchen table from me, stirring coffee so thin the milk he poured into it just turned it grey, and said, for the second or third time, "I swear, I don't remember seeing no Sue on the walls up there."

Kiki said, "Haw!"

7.

I covered the walls, with six inches of fiberglass insulation to help me through the winters, and then tongue-in-groove knotty pine, with which I did a pretty nice job for an amateur. I put in all new double-glazed windows; I patched the big hole in the floor and then laid a new floor over the whole thing, same pine as the walls; I put in a ceiling and spread a heavy layer of insulation over that, too; I hired a crew of highschool boys from town to help me haul my new wood-burning stove up the hill and set it in place. I left the repairs on the outhouse for another year, but I did a lot more on the cabin: put in a kitchen counter, sink, and drain; roughed in some shelving for cooking supplies and some for books and clothes; built a couple benches and chairs and even a bed frame; put some skirting around the base of the building to keep the wind from blowing up under the floor; added a new set of steps to the front; replaced some of the roof and then reshingled it all.

But I kept the door pretty much as it was.

Oh, I added big new hinges and strengthened the door frame and put weather-stripping all around it. I pounded some more nails into the door itself, for that matter, and squeezed caulking between all its planks to make certain it was good and wind-proof, and I added a new latch to hold it tight in the frame. I got a good deal of satisfaction, when I finally hung it, from the solid clunk it made when it swung into place in the frame.

Most of all, I liked the fact that from the inside I could still read, at right about eye level,

SUE

X

8.

One of the things that Sonny said he liked about the area was that when the Forestry Service had reopened it to logging, which had only happened gradually over the last couple decades, there hadn't been enough able-bodied men around to man a single crew for the companies who'd bid for and bought the rights to log in the State forests. The area had been pretty well logged over earlier in the century and then abandoned. There wasn't much else to keep people around, except for the tourist traffic in summer and the hunting and fishing in season and the usual incestuous commercial activity of the few towns scattered along the shore, people busy buying from and selling to each other. Labor had come along with the loggers, mostly from elsewhere around the state, accounting for the high proportion of Scandinavians in the current population here, but some from further off, including experienced loggers—mostly also Scandinavians, in all probability—the lumber companies moved in from the Northwest. Then the mining interests moved in, taking on the men who worked in the woods as the logging business dropped off, importing their own labor in boom years and in lean times dumping them back into the forests and incestuous towns, where they all soon learned other trades to cater to each other with.

"Get it?" Sonny said, "No old-timers."

"Just us," Kiki laughed. I knew they'd been here twenty years, ever since the first time they'd gotten married.

"So," I said, "nothing gets bound up with traditions?"

Sonny shook his head, splashed his pale coffee on the table. "Oh, there's ways of doing things here. It's not an easy place to live. You learn the way to do things or else. No, what I meant was, we're all newcomers here, just like you. There's no old-timers against new-comers, no us–them. Everybody's the same. Everybody gets an equal chance. For a while, at least."

"Got to be *some* old-timers," I argued. "Holdovers from the early logging days, those old Finns who thought they could farm the rocks and the ice, folks who run the tourist lodges, guys like the one who built my cabin. What about the Indians?"

Sonny shrugged. "They all get their chance, too. They're all the same."

"The Indians? The Indians got their chance? Sonny!" There were some issues on which Sonny and I never saw eye-to-eye and on which Kiki, like a traditional wife, kept her mouth shut. Not that theirs had exactly been a traditional marriage. Or marriages: they'd been divorced twice, returned to remarry each other both times. The first time, Sonny had moved down to the city for a few years. That was when I met him through mutual friends. We did a lot together. The second time it had been Kiki who moved to the city. She looked me up. Now they'd been back together for seven or eight years and nobody ever said anything about those times in the city. We were, as Sonny said, all newcomers here, though some of us, I thought, were newer newcomers than others. And others, I wanted to say, got better than equal chances, got more chances, even. But I knew what his answer to that would be: Made their chances. Had something to make them *with*, I would have coun-tered, something to make them *from*. Well shit, I could hear him say, any fool knows that nothin' never comes from nothin'.

"But what happens to them?" I pushed. "What happens to guys like the one who built my cabin?"

Sonny shrugged again, splashed a little more coffee on the formica tabletop. "Listen, there's somethin' I've been meaning to ask you."

"Oh, Sonny, leave him alone," Kiki said quietly, stirring the coffee she'd only sipped at, which must have gone quite cold by now.

"Just what the fuck are you planning on doing with yourself up there?"

9.

It was an interesting question, though I doubted the relevance of that last little "up there" phrase Sonny'd tacked on to it. In fact, I liked it stripped right down to its barest essentials: What the fuck are you doing? Not "Why are you doing that?" as my acquaintances in the city would have put it if I'd given them the chance, but the real question: What? "Why?" was rationalization and all my life I'd had my fill of that; as far as I could see, this was a century that had grown up on rationalization, on Freud and Marx and the like, and look where it had gotten us. "What?" was what happened, "What?" was history; and like any newcomer I was ready for some history.

I could hear Sonny's wry answer to that, too: You make it through a winter up there and you'll have all the history you want.

But the way I saw it, I was already acquiring some history. I had the cabin. I had "Sue."

And as to what I was doing, now that the cabin was pretty well finished I was cutting a lot of firewood, taking out nearby deadfalls, to start with, as long as they weren't rotted, and then thinning out some of the birch just over the edge of the ridge. The splitting could wait for the cold weather, when it'd be much easier, but for now I was piling up a good-sized supply of logs beside the cabin, that was what the fuck I was doing.

I didn't really figure it was going to take me much in the way of cash to get through the year. Sonny and Kiki seemed to need a fair amount, but then they had expensive habits, like being hooked up to the telephone and the power line, running a washer and dryer and TV set and two vehicles and the power tools in the basement where Sonny spent the winter turning out handcrafted knick-knacks to sell to the tourists in the summer. It was fairly amazing, the variety of ways in which he could turn thin birch slabs, which were available to him in an almost endless supply at almost no cost, into an instant source of cash. In addition, he had a small Army disability pension from the Korean War and was good enough with his hands to pretty much earn what he needed doing part-time plumbing and electrical work for local builders and even working in the summers at Urho's Standard, solving mechanical problems on tourists' cars and RVs while Kiki was home selling birch plaques. Kiki taught piano in the afternoons at the consolidated junior-senior high school and gave some private lessons at home in the evenings and on weekends. In the spring they both spent weekends working together, planting trees for the forest service, thousands and thousands of little seedlings in the areas that had been logged the season before. It was hard work, but it paid well, got them out-doors, and they liked doing it together. Sonny always said that Kiki was much the better at it because he always got distracted out there, looking at the spring wildflowers, finding animal tracks, pick-ing up interesting rocks. But I knew what a hard worker he was.

I figured I could do some tree-planting myself in the spring if I was really hard up for cash. I'd never done it before, but I'd never re-built an abandoned cabin before, either. I was making some history as I went along even though I wasn't, at the moment, making enough money to buy groceries with. The purchase of the land, rea-sonable as it was, plus the building supplies, which came pretty dear up here, had exhausted the savings account I'd managed to accumu-late over the years. I did have a paid-up, late-model car, and in Sonny a friend who could help me keep it running. I had a couple of articles out there that I'd written the previous winter and spring, pretty certain sales I thought, at airline magazines and the like, the sort of places I usually made my living from. If I didn't sell them to one, I'd sell them to another, eventually. And I had a fair chance for the part-time job that had just opened up on the local paper, fifty bucks a week for covering everything from church raffles to grade school track meets. It wasn't much, it certainly didn't qualify me for self-sufficiency, but I knew I could do a decent job for them if they'd give me the chance, and I knew I could get by on that.

Then if anybody asked what I was doing, I could say I was a newspaperman. A time-honored profession. That would save a lot of explaining that I wasn't sure I could do anyway.

10.

Not to say that going off to a cabin in the woods wasn't itself a time-honored profession. Maybe "profession" is a little strong. Time-honored idea, then. Or if not idea, perhaps possibility, alternative, option. Notion, at the very least. And, granted, a notion more honored in the classroom than in the woods. Particularly in these woods. There is no sense planting a bean patch here, the growing season is too short. The idealism of this notion begins to wither as soon as you realize that you have to spend most of the spring, summer, and fall putting up firewood for the winter, which is most of the year. Your bean-patch philosopher does not, in such circumstances, have a lot of time to let his mind stalk the forest of ideas, at least not till winter sets in, and then his major idea is likely to be survival. Survival is hauling the firewood you spent the three brief seasons felling and cutting, keeping the fire going, making the heavy treks out for supplies and back in again, laden down with as much as you can carry, melting snow for water and keeping some sort of path open to the outhouse, splitting frozen logs, shoveling out ashes, pulling the snow load off the roof, trying to boost the larder by doing a little ice-fishing when you get time. Is there really a history to such a life? Could anyone ever really consider such a life to be a time-honored profession or even a noble idea? An odd or dismal notion maybe. A necessity of the times, perhaps, for some, at certain times. Sonny would have laughed, Kiki snorted, at Thoreau, if they had ever heard of him. I, for one, have never mentioned his name north of the forty-fifth parallel.

In spite of which, in spite of Sonny and Kiki's hilarity and the fine spray of grey coffee the three of us would doubtless precipitate across the kitchen table at the climax of such a discussion, I would be the last to deny that going off to a cabin in the woods does indeed have a long and interesting history. Look at this very cabin in the woods in which I am now living and, public records to the contrary, you cannot deny history. I have been to the county courthouse and discovered that, though this parcel of land has passed through half a dozen hands in the past century, from Laaskinen, Elmo, to myself, on no occasion (including the present) was a building permit ever issued, as required by law, for the construction (or reconstruction) of a warehouse, a business, an office, a domicile, or a seasonal dwelling of any sort. And yet I can right now reach across the desk on which I am writing (cedar planks, cedar legs, and cedar crossbraces, from the cedars of this very land) and rap on the paneling of this very sturdy wall behind which, and beyond six inches of fiberglass insulation, is carved in solid cedar the name of a previous visitor to this building which the county does not even record as existing. She has passed into, become a part of, its history, and though to some neither she nor the building exists, and to others whether they exist or not they are suspect, I, who have added my own layering to both, respect them both. Such respect, I have found, actually takes very little in the way of time and effort, and can be done while splitting logs, snowshoeing down the trail, or frying eggs on a wood cookstove.

Such respect is easy, I think, because it demands so little in the way of understanding, which is, to be sure, often hard. Thanks to certain of our intellectual ancestors in the last century, we have become very big on understanding in this one. But not only is that sort of understanding a Johnny-come-lately whose worth is yet to be proven, the fact is that whatever its value, it cannot be reached by leaping over what came before. What came before was respect, simple respect. Respect has a history which cannot be bypassed. I doubt if it is ever possible to arrive at any understanding without, to begin with, respect for the object of that hoped-for understanding. Since we are all newcomers here, we have got to begin by respecting what was here before us. Sue. The cabin. This whole wintry region. Because that is what is here.

II.

I have asked rather widely about in the community now that I have become a part of it, and no one knows who built this cabin originally or why or how long ago. No one knows how long the original builder lived here and whether alone or not or the reason the place was finally abandoned or even whether anyone took up residence here later on, before me. They are all newcomers and, like me, they know nothing. Many, even many who know of the lake, did not know of the cabin's existence, though they are generally quick to admire both the effort its construction must have taken and its powers of endurance. Some few even admire my own efforts in reconstructing it and moving in here, though most of the men I drink coffee with in Karen's Kafe, when I make my treks for supplies into town by snowshoe and snow-tired car, are inclined to wonder like Sonny—though on the whole a little more euphemistically—perhaps because their sisters and daughters are roaming the Kafe serving them watery coffee—what the fuck I am doing up there.

If I told them about Sue—which I do not, because, as the County Recorder's office attests, not all history is public history—I do not think they would wonder what the fuck she was doing up there. I am sure that they would feel quite certain that they knew exactly what Sue was doing up there. With a laugh or a sly joke and perhaps a glance of uncertainty at the women moving among the tables with steaming pots of coffee, they would, like most people I know, lay claim to an easy understanding of what Sue was doing up at that abandoned cabin. But I, even I who have Sue's name emblazoned on my door and preserved behind my walls, do not claim such an understanding. Neither do I think that understanding is what's called for here, because I do not think that understanding is what can be had. No more than Sue herself, whom none of us ever knew.

Not for a moment can we begin to understand the complexities of life that led Sue up to this cabin on even the first occasion when she left her name behind – no more than we can know which one of these sets of carvings that surrounds me, if any, represents that first occasion. Oh, we can joke about the simplicities of what led her here, but on the complexities we can't even begin to speculate. And to go for the simplicities is not to understand, to simplify is not to have anything of either Sue or her history, or even the cabin's, but only to have our own simplifications. That's not history, that's not respect, that's most certainly not Sue. We can speculate readily enough upon a fact of history, and

SUE

X

BOBBY

is indeed just such a fact, but that is all it is, just a single, simple fact. It is not history. And such a fact of history we can probably do little of value with. We can gossip about the facts or otherwise amuse ourselves with them; we can put them together in all their various possible combinations, thereby showing off the agility of our own minds but demonstrating little about history except its vulnerability; and just as easily we can malign or even falsify the facts. But the fact is not understanding. It is not history, neither the cabin's nor Sue's. A fact is just a fact, though one might be well-advised to omit the "just." It is a fact that I have spent the winter here, but what of it? My acquaintances in the city will find it amusing, something to chat about and puzzle over. They will think that if they could only sit me down over drinks and ask me "Why?" and what led to my decision to do such a thing, then they would understand everything. They would understand nothing, not even when I answered their "Why?" by telling them, "Because it is now part of my history." My friends, on the other hand, would not ask me "Why?" They would welcome me to the city when I came to visit and give me hugs of farewell when I left to return to my cabin. They would listen to what I had done, was doing, and would respect it. As I think they would also respect Sue.

12.

Sue. For all his doubt about her very existence and his gentle cynicism about my life here, I will let the final word be Sonny's because of what he said when he finally paid me a visit here, late in the spring. It was May, the south slopes of the gullies still held the snow, and, chainsaw roaring, I was already working on my new supply of firewood for the coming winter. The saw was so noisy he came up on me unheard, seemed simply to be there, standing watching me at work with his hands in his pockets. Though the birches had begun to leaf out and some early wildflowers had made their appearance, it was a chilly day, and I motioned Sonny to go inside the cabin. I wanted to show him the place. I wanted to sit and talk with him about it and pour him good strong coffee of my own brewing. He went on in while I shut off the chainsaw and laid it on top of the woodpile and kicked the mud off my boots. I could hear Kiki now, still coming up the trail on the other side of the ridge, whistling. Inside, I found Sonny standing dead center in the cabin, looking at me as I entered, overheated from cutting logs, pulling my denim jacket off. Only I realized right away he wasn't looking at me but at the inside of the door, where Sue's name was carved, with the blank below.

"So," he said, not questioningly like some people would have done but just making a flat-out statement: "that's Sue."

Composition in Perpetua by Annie Graham. Designed by Allan Kornblum. Printed at McNaughton & Gunn. This book was printed on acid-free paper, and was sewn in signatures to insure durability.